Wyldblood

Issue 11 - Winter 2023

In This Issue:

Wyldblood Magazine #11, Spring 2023
ISBN-978-1-914417-14-6
© 2023 Wyldblood Press and contributors.

Publisher: Wyldblood Press, Thicket View, Bakers Lane, Maidenhead SL6 6PX UK. www.wyldblood.com **Editor:** Mark Bilsborough. **Fiction editor** Sandra Baker. **Subscriptions:** 6 issues epub/mobi/pdf delivered to your inbox £18. 6 issue print subscriptions £30. Single issues available worldwide via Amazon and from wyldblood.com/shop **Issue 12 will be published in April 2023**

Submissions: we are regularly open for submissions of flash fiction, short stories and novels – check our website for our current status and requirements. We are a paying market. We also need artwork, people to review us, and people to review *for* us. Email contact@wyldblood.com

Editorial

Mark Bilsborough

Welcome to Wyldblood 11 – our first issue of 2023. I, for one, am glad to see the back of 2022 (though it was undoubtedly a good one for Wyldblood Press) with its endless stream of bad news about war, Covid, the economy and politics (through I guess that depends on your view of how the Midterms went. In the UK we managed three Prime Ministers in less than three months, leaving the battered wreckage of our economy trailing in the wake of the second one, and now everyone's on strike trying to claw back some of the damage to their wages). But I'm in danger of getting political, which is something we've always tried to avoid at Wyldblood, because we're conscious that not all science fiction and fantasy readers think like we do, and it's not for us to judge.

That's a hard place to be, sometimes. We've currently sitting on an extraordinarily good story that we've been discussing not taking because it's got a strong political position. It's one that we happen to wholeheartedly agree with, but it's a polarising narrative (as seems to be the case with many things in politics these days). But are we being naïve in thinking we can publish without offending someone, somewhere? The history of science fiction and fantasy is littered with political positions, from Tolkein's extended rant against industrialisation in *Lord of the Rings* through Robert Heinlein's increasingly right-wing libertarian heroes and the blatant political allegories that characterised early *Star Trek*. And they're all good stories, even if we may not agree with some of the sentiments they express. Expressing a view on anything is political in some way – avoiding taking a position on anything would lead to some very strange (and probably boring) stories. So we're going to publish the story.

But I do worry about only publishing stories that agree with us politically. We'll try not to do that – good stories should always be welcome in our pages, even if we don't agree with the message (and we can always add a disclaimer). But I doubt we'll be taking any climate change denying stories anytime soon.

We recently published or first 'Best of' collection (with stories from our first eight issues) and it feels like we're in phase 2 now – not the new kids on the block anymore but still with a point to prove. So this next year will be a time of consolidation and steady expansion. Look out for novellas, podcasts, our *From the Depths* anthology and three more issues of Wyldblood Magazine before the year's out.

This time around we've got stories about redundant princesses (what do you do next?), colony ships (what have you left behind?), clones (and how to kill them), surviving the dystopia, a disembodied hand, the irresistible lure of virtual reality and much, much more.

Mark

Bronze

Richard Strachan

But a man must eat, he thought.

He pared back the skin and cut away a piece of meat, the high sweet smell of rot feathering the air in front of him. Other animals had been at the deer's carcass already, and there were maggots frothing from its eyes. A strong flame and the meat burnt black as charcoal - it would have to do. In the light that dappled from the broken canopy the deer's hide was striped and patched with ragged lines of shadow; a foot more to his left and he wouldn't have seen it, and then his day would have been fuelled on nothing more than a picking of berries, a handful of wild mushroom and a shard of bark. He gave up his prayer of thanks and looked over his shoulder to see what might come to claim it.

He put flint to firestone by a heap of dried leaves and dead wood, and before long the smoke was rising. He cut and skewered cubes of the scavenged meat and held them above the flames, watching the cool yellow tongues lap at them, the juice of their corruption boiling and hissing in the fire, just as the water hissed against the shore on the other side of the treeline and across the pebbled sands. He ate, licking the grease from his fingers. As he lay down to sleep he tried to ignore the roiling in his gut and the lean pains that moved behind his ribs. In the dance of the firelight he stared towards the deeper woods. He'd be safe here, this close to shore. They didn't come this far out.

In the morning he felt better, fitter, and obscurely proud of the constitution that could keep such rank fare down. He rolled up his blanket and slung it over his shoulder, hefted the fox hide knapsack and tucked the flint knife into his belt where his hand could pluck it free. There was no trail to follow this far into the trees, but at the same time he didn't want to stray too near the open ground. He picked his way over the roots and the tough, unyielding thickets of grey grass, through sheets of ground ivy and the great dripping sprays of fern. A thin rain began to fall, salt-scented from the sea, a smear of moisture in the air. He could feel it prickling against his beard. Somewhere off to his right, heard even above the quickening mumble of the leaves, was the low resounding boom of the waves. Painted people on one side, he thought, and the Bound Men on the other …

The knife was in his hand before he'd even thought to draw it, the flint's tapering blade angled outwards while he dropped into a half-crouch. Peering so long at the cross-cut jumble of the

3

forest, the wavering greens and browns of the branches and the leaves, his eyes had latched onto anything that stood out, and nothing stood out here as much as a man's face. Or in this case, he realised, a girl's.

She was young, no more than eleven or twelve summers, and she was sobbing quietly in a clearing just ahead. The grey light softened the distance between them, and he could see where the drizzle had wetted the girl's face between the tears.

'Have you travelled far?' the nameless man said, stepping into the clearing. He slid the knife away. When two met on strange trails there was no easy way to fall into the encounter without causing at least some alarm, so best to step boldly, he thought, and show open hands.

The girl reared back, as he knew she would, but she didn't run. She stumbled over the fallen trunk she'd been leaning against and flapped an arm back to shift the grey roughspun from her shoulder, but there was no weapon at her side. She was wearing a thin white robe beneath the cloak, stained and ragged, but had no bag, no blanket, and her feet were bare and bloody.

'What's your name girl?' the man asked. He had none to give in exchange. He moved carefully, stooping to seem less large. Although not tall he had at least a head and a half over this child. He sat opposite on the flayed trunk of another dead tree and from his knapsack took his few remaining berries, a handful of dried mushrooms. 'I've nothing to cook them in or we could have had ourselves some soup. Do you like soup? I'd give an arm for soup.'

For the first time that day he set to building a fire, taking the kindling from the dry depths of his knapsack and casting around for sticks. A grey wet day now, but the clearing was mostly sheltered. He said nothing more, aware of the girl watching him, following the motion of the sparks as he struck the little nub of flint to the firestone. In the light the flecks of gold glowed a dull and buttery yellow, but as the sparks took hold they roared with colour. Soon the flames were crackling pleasantly, hissing in the rain as the drippings from the meat had hissed last night, the first piece of meat he'd had for days …

Before long, to no great surprise, the girl came closer and crouched by the fire. She held her hands out to warm them, warily considering the man through the flames.

'Are you going to tell me your name? Or should I just call you "girl" as long as we're in company.'

'Elsbeth.' She shuffled and crossed her legs on the damp ground. 'Although they called me an Oracle. One who knows.'

'One who knows what? Where to find food? A useful skill if you're as bad a hunter as me.' He passed over the berries and mushrooms. 'And not much of a forager either, if we're telling truths around this fire. No fighter,' he sighed, 'no taleteller, no bard, no leader of men, and too young to be an elder … Perhaps I don't have much to offer, but I do have my berries, and I do have a way with a fire.'

'They would have burned me,' Elsbeth said. 'If I hadn't run. They were going to burn me.'

'Here's this "they" again.'

'But I ran.' She looked at her hands. 'All those years and I never knew their names. They were so kind to me though, all of them. They were kind men ...'

'Eat,' the man said. The girl shovelled the food into her mouth and chewed with her eyes closed, a string of spit leaking from the corner of her lips. When she had finished, washing it down with the brackish water from the skin the nameless man passed to her, she told him who they were. The Bound Men, she said. The grey priests of the shore.

There had always been the cave. She couldn't remember anything before it. She couldn't remember her mother or her father or where she might have been born, if anywhere. All she could remember were the kindly men who cared for her, who made sure that the fire was bright and the deerskin across the cave mouth was thick enough to shelter her; who saw that she was well fed and watered, and that as she was growing up she had toys to play with - a carved and impish face on an oval of polished bone, a little hazelwood figure lashed together with green twine. All through the months and years they came, every day, to check on her and make sure she was happy, and then once a month they would come to ask the question.

'I always got the question right,' Elsbeth said. 'And they were always so pleased with me. They were so pleased, they would wait outside the cave and come in one at a time to hold me, and tell me how good I was, how good I must be the next month. I got it right every time … but in the end I got it wrong.'

The cave where she lived, where she grew up, was in a sheer outcrop of rock that jutted into the sea. Sometimes she would wake with the salt spray on her lips, mingling with that other taste, the essence of the priests. All through the night she'd listen to the wild music, the boom and repeat of the breaking waves, or on softer days their whisper, that light shushing sound as the water mingled with the sand and stones. She dreamed the song of the sea, and she could hear it now, she said, as they sat by the guttering fire in this low clearing. She knew every shade of its appearance as well, the way the far waves would loom above the surface in one great curling fist and shatter in the deep, a cascade of white spray catching in the sun like a handful of thrown jewels.

'Like the gold in your firestone,' Elsbeth told him. 'Or even like the light inside the fire.'

On quiet days it was something different again, a smooth unrolling that wobbled and swayed to the unseen beat of the wind, green and blue and lit by darker patches as the clouds unfolded above. She'd step from the cave and see that slack expanse, and looking back would see the dark sweep of forest in the distance, haunt of the Painted People and death to anyone who crossed it. She felt glad for the sea. Rather the sea than the trees, the grey priests said. She felt a sister to those waters, and sometimes she'd even be so bold as to walk up to the waves, the creamy fluttering of the foam as it bubbled on the sand, feeling the cold kiss of them against her bare feet. She wondered if she'd ever had a sister before. Then, once a month, she would stand in the cave mouth and watch the Bound Men in their long grey robes process along the shore towards her, the scented smoke erupting from their bowls of clay and stone, and even above the sound of the waves came their muffled chanting. Each time they gathered together like this and journeyed from their huts and the stone altars, she would feel her stomach lurch at the thought that she might not be able to answer. But it was always the same, that's what she couldn't understand. For as long as she could remember anything, the question and the answer were always the same.

As she talked, the girl didn't meet the man's eyes, and the man knew enough to understand that the girl wasn't so much telling the story as reciting it. She was fitting together all the scraps and pieces of her experience, placing the shapes next to each other to see if they fit, and if any of them made sense either apart or in total. How many years had Elsbeth spent with the Bound Men, he wondered? From the sounds of it her whole life. He knew they paid well for children, for infants gifted from the breast, or given shelter when a mother died in birthing. For some it was the only hope of life, to be taken in as an oracle by the grey priests, and to have this question put to them all their lives. Or most of their lives, at least … As he listened to the girl he knew not to press the issue on what the question might have been. The girl's dark eyes had drifted back into the sight of his old life, which should have ended in the flames, and now settled on this different fire; here inside the trees, where none came but the painted ones, in the chance company of some half-starved stranger. What would I tell her about myself, the man thought. What are the pieces of my experience but failure, and low birth, and women who all turn away from me. A man with no good name, who now goes nameless.

He stoked the fire with a stick. This cold that gathered, this coastal chill, there seemed nothing that could soften it.

'The foolish thing is,' Elsbeth went on, 'they told me what to say from the beginning, when I was a girl and too slow to know what it was they were asking. "Will the tides come?" they said, and they'd nod their heads until I nodded mine and said "Yes." Every month, just that. "Will the tides come?", and I'd look out to sea and wonder how they could not?'

There were other questions, the man knew, but he wondered if the girl did. Up and down the coast, there were girls and priests and questions. "Will the rain fall?" "Will the sun rise?" "Will the grass grow?" Yes, yes, and always yes. No, it was not well done, not at all. But how else was the sun supposed to rise? How else did the grass grow, and the tides come? It was as it had to be.

Later in the afternoon they walked on through the forest, keeping the line of shore always in sight through its bristling barrier of trees; close enough so that they could run for the safety of the open if they needed to, or run deeper into the trees if that seemed the wiser course.

The girl had fallen in with him, as he knew she would. Stepping carefully on her painful feet through the undergrowth, sweeping the bracken aside where it frothed up from the darker ground, trailing long rags of ground ivy, Elsbeth stumbled after. Every step seemed to lighten her mood; that and the handful of berries she'd eaten. As they walked, she kept looking off into the deeper growth on their left, where the trees crept closer together and the darkness between them was broken by no shaft of sunlight. Nervously she looked, but with a kind of dark attraction too - what child didn't thrill to the tales of the patchwork men, half-gods and half-ghosts; even a child raised in a cave, and raised by the grey priests of the shore.

'Are they real?' Elsbeth asked the man. She wiped a dirty hand across her dirty face and pulled at her formerly white robes. The nameless man knew who she meant.

'Real enough.'

'I've heard of them. The kindly men, the fathers, told me never to leave the cave and never to go into the forest. They said ...'

'Go on then, what did they say? I've heard it all myself.'

'They said you'd never see them until they were on you. That they scarred their skin and stained it with all the dyes of the forest, and that if one was to stand an arm's length from you, you'd never see him till he blinked his eyes, all painted with the colours of the trees, and the shadows, and the light.'

'That's true enough,' the man said. Looking to his left, he fished for a sight of them. But of course you wouldn't see. They could be right there and you wouldn't catch a sight of them.

'Cannibals as well, they eat their young and they only keep one baby in three,' Elsbeth said, scurrying to catch up. She seemed almost cheerful now; the boundless and unbreakable resilience of the young. A whole life under the Bound Men, and then having to run into the forest to escape a death by burning, and all it takes is half a handful of berries and a stranger's company to make her scamper like a child. 'They're not men or women, but both somehow, and in the middle of the forest there's a tree that's wider than the biggest village you've ever seen, with doors and windows and tunnels underneath it, and inside they pray to a giant fungus to help them with their leaf magic, and they can bind the pelts of animals to their skin and -'

'The priests said all this to you?'

'As good as. They said they were here first, before any of us. That they've always been here.'

'Some say they'll be here last, when the rest of us have gone. Others say they're not really here at all, and that they're looking back at us from a world we can't imagine, and everything we do is just a dream inside the mind of the painted folk.'

The girl digested this for a moment. 'When the rest of us have gone where?'

'Wherever the land goes when it dies, and all the people in it.'

The girl fell back then, solemn and contemplative, and when next the man looked round she was crouching by the stump flare of a swollen pine, rummaging in the undergrowth at its base.

'What is it?' the man said. 'Elsbeth? What have you found?'

The girl stood and held it out, and the man took it from her; a foot of finger-thin wood, pale green like a branching shoot, and straight as an –

'It's one of theirs, isn't it?' Elsbeth said. The man nodded. On the unfletched end of the arrow was the split where the head should have been, the barbed oval or the leaf-shaped little blade. Bone or flint, he suspected, or fired wood, but he'd heard they used bronze as well. He'd heard they used more than that, a metal wreathed in magics so bright you could see your face in it, so strong it would never break, but he didn't believe that for a moment. More tales. What he wouldn't give to see real bronze though, if the patchwork folk didn't always gather back their points.

He was about to tuck the arrow shaft into his belt when an older voice inside him said 'No.' He cast it back into the weeds.

'Let's press on,' he said. 'It'll be dark soon.'

To that night's campfire the man came from the hunt with a brown lizard missing its tail and two speckled eggs from the nest of a redshank near the shore. The waves had been lapping at its borders, and by high tide he knew the water would be in amongst the trees. It was wrong, he thought. It shouldn't be like this. Something is very, very wrong. He'd never known the sea so swollen; there seemed more of it every day, and he'd heard travellers speak of the ice mountains melting in the north, the great glaciers just crumbling into wet pieces and the melt trickling into the valleys beneath them. He'd never seen it for himself, but then he'd never been as far as he wanted. There was so much that he hadn't seen, that he'd failed to do. You walked for a year and it never felt enough.

While they ate the girl looked at him over the dancing flame.

'When I first saw you,' she said, 'I thought you were one of them. Just at first, when you stepped into the clearing.'

'They would never be so bold,' he said. Elsbeth laughed. 'And if you had seen one, we wouldn't be sitting here now, would we?'

'Where is it you're going? I feel I've interrupted you, and I never thought to ask.'

'Nowhere. Anywhere,' the man said. He stretched out on his blanket by the fire. 'Wherever my stomach leads me.'

'I hadn't thought about it before,' Elsbeth said. She was in no mood to sleep, the man saw. 'Food, and how to get it. The priests always brought me everything I needed.' She curled up on the ground, and when she spoke the words seemed to come from the wild depths of the flames between them. 'Suppose I'll *have* to start thinking about it now. Food, and how to get it ...'

'They're harsh masters, the Bound Men,' he said. 'But they're fair to their own.'

Generous to the girls in their care, he thought. But harsh masters indeed if the answers were not to their liking.

He lay there by the fire, listening to it crackle and snarl, and he thought of the Bound Men, the grey priests of the shore who helped hold the world together. What would they make of the rising tides, the rain, the heat in winter and the cold of summer? How would they stop the valleys flooding? How many girls would burn to put it right?

Suddenly he was cold, as if the fire was casting out all the grey and silver light of the melting ice. As if she had been following his thoughts, the girl said:

'I woke early that day, like I knew it was my last. I stood by the mouth of the cave and watched them come along the shore, ten of them, in a line. The grey robes and their grey hair trailing out behind them, and the waves licking up against their ankles. They were singing. The smoke was thick about them. I remember they clambered up the rocks towards me and one of them fell, skinning his palm. Then I sat and waited for them to ask, and without even thinking about it, for the first time in my life, I gave them the wrong answer. But it was only wrong because it was *true*.'

Will the tides come? the man thought. He could almost hear the words, and the answer that followed. *No ... There is no tide now but the rising sea.*

After that they had dragged her from the cave onto the rocks. She pointed but they wouldn't see. They threw her back inside, and a day later led her from the cave mouth to the narrowing stretch of beach, the strip of sand and pebble where the pyre was high and ready, the flames licking around the torches in their hands as they leaned in for the burning.

Maybe they hadn't thought one of their girls would run. Obedient to the last, many of them walked willingly to their deaths. But Elsbeth had run. Sister to the sea, heir of that wild power, she had kicked and bitten as they tied her to the stake, punching and flailing out at the kindly fathers who would kill her, and she ran until the heart was heaving in her chest, ran towards the black woods and the patchwork men, who couldn't possibly be as dangerous as the men who had raised her.

'Then I found you,' Elsbeth said. Between them the flames of the campfire flickered and died.

He'd forgotten what it was like to talk so much, and he didn't have the girl's skill with it. He imagined Elsbeth hadn't said much more than that single 'Yes' once a month for years, and the pent up need to speak was bursting from her. It was something to think as they set off walking next morning; the experiences that went together to make a person, and the person you always were inside, from the beginning. They said your life was set out from the moment you were born, but he had never believed that. How could even the gods above keep a fraction of the chances that went into a man's life straight in their minds? There was only what felt good and what felt bad, and there was only luck. Here was this girl, whose luck was bad, and look at her, singing and slashing at the undergrowth with a stick - she acted now as if life was something to be enjoyed.

'If you don't know where you're going, then why not say where you're from?' Elsbeth asked him. 'I'd try to guess, but the fathers never told me much of what was beyond the shore, and I don't know any further than the next village. One said once that there were lands beyond the sea, is that true? Blasphemous men take big ships and travel there, to dark lands that are filled with devils.'

'I wouldn't know about dark lands or devils, but there are other places beyond it. That I've heard, anyway. I don't know. I've always lived near the shore myself.'

'You're from here?'

'Not here, but further along. Many weeks of walking along, past this end of the forest.'

'It has an end?'

The nameless man laughed. 'It has two.'

'So what's on the other side?'

'Another shore.'

He wondered if he should say. What harm would it do.

'I've talked to men who've been across the seas,' he said, 'and men who've travelled far. There are cities out there, they say, gatherings of villages all in one place, hundreds of them end to end, and around them tall walls made of stone. Have you ever seen bronze, girl? I don't suppose you have.'

'I've never even heard of it.'

'It's metal. Metal that doesn't bend, and makes a blade sharper than you could believe. And brighter too, when it's polished up, brighter than the sun striking the water on the hottest day of the year. There are some over there across the sea who know how to make it.'

'How?'

'You're asking the wrong man. They do something with the copper, far as I know, but I couldn't tell you what.'

He held out the flint blade for the girl to see.

'This serves, as it always has, but when all men have bronze who'll keep a stone as their blade? I think that's what your fathers didn't like when you answered them wrong. They knew change was on the way, a mighty change they couldn't begin to imagine, and they hated it.'

The trees were thinning out now, and in the spaces between them rose their twisted roots and the wildflowers that were kissed with light from the opening canopy. Grass rustled in a smooth sea breeze.

'Here,' he said. 'Look. We're coming to the end of it.' The girl looked, and before they stepped out of the forest the man said, 'I saw one once myself. Many years ago.'

'One of the painted folk?'

'A patchwork man. Just for a moment. I wasn't much older than you are now and I was gathering wood with my father. It's true what they say - they could be a foot in front of you and you wouldn't know it until they blinked.'

He thought back to it, the memory that was fully-fleshed within him no matter how many years had passed. He felt again the dry wood in his hands and heard his father crunching through the undergrowth some way ahead. In the soft summer air he could smell the black medick and the mallow on the edge of the trees, where the hazels spilled out onto the couch grass and the low dunes of the shoreline. His father, whistling away, and his bare feet with the soles as hard as horn.

He had been deeper into the forest than he realised. The light was slackening and the air was thick with wood dust and pollen, and a feeling had begun to catch at him in its mellow fingers. Standing there heavy-headed, pleasurably numb, his scalp buzzing, he realised that he was staring at a patch of forest in front of him. He stared, and he looked, and then he *looked* … And there in the tangle of light and shade, the latticework of branch and leaf, all that greenery formed before him into something like a face. There was a body beneath it, he felt, not much taller than him but thickset and powerful, and light and fleeting at the same time. Around its eyes and mouth were broken lines of green, copper and black, great streaks of forest colours, the eyes above them staring gold and bright. There was no malice in it, he had thought. This is kindness, or something older than kindness, but before he could say a word or even frame to himself what it was he was seeing he felt a finger of its thought reach out and touch him, just for a heartbeat of time …

Then his father called his name, and when he looked back it was gone.

The forest held no fear for him since that day. When his friends skirted its borders or piously averted their eyes from the trees, he had just laughed and plunged in, never going too far, always keeping a respectful distance. After today though, he could never come back. They would know. They would reach out, and they would *know*.

Elsbeth followed him as he walked onto the shore, the sea humming fretfully before them, the whitecaps further out erupting into curls and columns of spray. The sky was a thick grey above it, and when Elsbeth saw the Bound Men patiently waiting by their pyre she turned and tried to run. The nameless man caught her quickly, lifting her and tucking her under his arm, and with a great band of pain coiled around his forehead, his teeth bared, he dragged the girl down towards the sea.

They gave him salt fish, as much as he could carry, dried apples too, and bladderwrack gathered from the shore. He filled his knapsack and waited with his heart fluttering in his chest. He caught his breath when they gave him the dagger.

Bronze. So sharp he cut his finger when he laid it lightly against the blade.

He left before the burning. The forest was at his back, and on his right the sea was shattering itself against the rocks. But a man must *eat*, he said. The wind took his words towards the trees.

Richard Strachan is an Edinburgh-based writer and has had stories in magazines like Interzone, The Lonely Crowd, Gutter *and* New Writing Scotland, *and recently had stories accepted for* Metaphorosis Magazine *and the 'Midnight in the Dying Garden' anthology, He's also published a number of novels and short stories for Games Workshop's Black Library imprint, set in their Warhammer worlds.*

Last Chance Lottery

Michael Teasdale

"...happily, ever after."

Keema lets her index finger brush across the page, tracing the words, letting them tumble from her lips with a quiet tenderness that can barely be heard over the steady, undulating thrum of the ark. She seldom catches the sound during the day, where it creeps into her consciousness only sporadically; like the mild disturbance of a soft, faraway breeze, barely detectable over the general commotion of the people and the chaos of their lives.

At night, however, it filters slowly back into her cognizance until it becomes all that she can hear. Its reverberations pull her mind down through the reinforced titanium floors, sinking deep into the bowels of the craft. Delving into the unseen spaces that neither Keema nor her fellow passengers ever glimpse in the artificial light of day. It is here, in these sealed off secret spaces, that the sound takes shape. Keema remembers the explanation from her orientation week and can still recall the dry monotone voice of the speaker, explaining how the ark's ramjet scoop siphons the hydrogen particles, tearing them free from the solar winds that carry the craft on its exodus. Keema doesn't fully understand the intricacies of the science, knowing only that the particles power everything, from the ark's life support systems to the little electric mobile that hangs above Ellie's cot.

Closing the book quietly, not wanting to disturb her sleeping daughter, she lowers her gaze, letting it linger on the quilted green scales of the book-cover. The friendly, googly eyes of the dragon, a forgotten fantasy from a world left behind, stare back at her and she gives the tome a little shake, suppressing a giggle as the dragon's eyes roll in response.

It is here, in these silent, night-time hours that Keema finds her inner-peace. When the ship grows quiet, when the shops and restaurants close and shutter for the day. When the entertainment halls empty and the passengers spill back into to their sleeping quarters. When the energy and noise of the day settles into stillness, like a bizarro butterfly crawling back into its cocoon and melding into the quiet, reassuring throb of the craft. The sound, the steady white noise of an airplane cabin of old, brings with it comfort, a sign that all is calm. By the time the lights dim, she can almost pretend that things are normal.

Placing the book carefully on the little nightstand, Keema lets her eyes rest on the slumbering shape in the cot. The story of the dragon and its search for a home is something Ellie seemingly never tires of. Yet, for all she loves it, the sleep usually takes her long before Keema reaches the end.

"Dwagon, Mama. Dwagon." The same request, every evening. And Keema smiles, takes the book down from the shelf and begins the tale over.

"Once upon a time…"

"The words aren't important, Keema." The ship psychologist tells her during one of their weekly sessions, "It's hearing your voice that matters. We want Ellie to experience as normal a childhood as possible. Heck! it's important for *you* that this is a normal motherhood. When you're with her, on the infant deck, just try to tune everything else out."

'Normal.' It's *an interesting word,* thinks Keema.

She, takes the advice anyway, shaking her head clear of errant thoughts as she leans over the crib, peeking at Ellie. Her daughter lies on her back, fast asleep, with the blanket pulled up to the tip of her button nose. Keema watches from under the pinkish glow of the nightlight as the child's eyelids flutter in the staccato rhythm of REM. She lets her hands spread out over the warm cotton of the blanket and spends a moment tucking her daughter in, before her gaze wanders up to the little decoration that hangs above the cot. The brightly coloured rocket wobbles as it follows the orbit of the unknown planet, moving in a slow circular procession above them, never quite catching up with its intended target.

Most of the other moms on the infant deck favor the standard holo-projections that their quarters come equipped with, yet Ellie has never taken to those like she has with this traditional artifact; this cheaply made thing of plastic and chipped paint.

The mobile was gifted to her, a few weeks ago, by a kind-eyed, tired looking mom from across the corridor, after Ellie had woken crying for the third time in the same night.

"Here," the woman said, handing over the decoration "Sam used to scream the place down at her age until I got him this. After I put it up, he'd lie there like he was hypnotized. Who can figure out why they like these old things so much, but it does the trick! I think the sensitive ones can tell that the holograms aren't real. They're looking for something solid they can reach for. You take it dear and I hope it helps. You look like you could use a good night's shut-eye."

Ever since that day, Ellie has slept like a charm, but Keema still finds that her own brain won't settle. Her thoughts refuse to shut down in the manner the psychologist suggests that they ought to. She can spend the days operating on autopilot, but at night all the memories of the time before come flooding back and she finds herself lost in invisible conversations, muttering snatches of half-remembered dialogue to people she once knew, invoking old arguments, reliving old loves. Trapped in a relentless discourse with the lost things of her past.

Now, when she does sleep, her dreams are disappointingly empty, as if her brain hasn't yet figured out how to interpret the new reality of her life.

The ship's therapist suggested that the night walks might be a useful outlet and Keema has been taking them regularly ever since, even if the dreams still don't come.

Now it is almost time again.

She slides her all-purpose-device out from her pocket and drags her index finger across the screen, activating cabin security mode. In the corner of the ceiling, a green light begins blinking and Keema waves at the invisible eyes now monitoring her from a distant security room.

"Sleep tight, Princess" she mouths, as she tiptoes backward across the carpet and over to the nearby wall which dilates in response; a previously invisible door blinking silently open. She pauses only to blow a kiss to Ellie, then steps through the portal and out into the corridor, letting the door slide seamlessly closed, while her mind drifts into the memory of an altogether different time and place.

Keema, nineteen and carefree, gazes up at the impossible brightness of tonight's full moon. Wriggling her toes, she buries them into the cool, wet Koh Pha Ngan sands. She feels the heat of the flame on her sun-kissed face, breathes in the sweet sting of the liquor as the firebreather billows out a small, uncontrollable inferno just a few feet away.

The nearby crowd whoop in excitement; a mass of writhing subtle young bodies, all toned abs and minuscule bikinis, smeared with phosphorescent body-paint. It is a gaudy tribute to the youth of a century past, now revered in retrospect as the carefree children of a more innocent age. Here they dance, illuminated as a living Edvard Munch painting, hollering against the backdrop of black crashing waves that rush to devour the pale sands at their naked feet. They are innocence lost forever, raging at the dying of the light. Rebel angels abandoned by a God who never showed up to his own party.

A smaller burst of orange pulls Keema's attention to the left, where a young Thai boy is juggling fiery skittles. The batons are real, the flames are not simulations as they once would have been. Everything here is recreated for posterity, not sanitised for their protection. This is the point of the gathering. The last chance of a doomed generation to experience the rawness of life as it once was and never will be again.

Keema smiles as she watches the boy's confidence grow, twirling the batons high into the air. The crowd roars him on and a drunk farang girl gets too close to him as she tries to snap a picture on her APD. The boy is distracted by the girl's raw beauty, he stumbles on a half-buried beer bottle. An older man, carrying a balloon and a strange looking cannister, looks on nervously as the boy loses control of a baton. There is a gasp as the skittle leaves its predicted arc, veering off instead toward an area where a group of riotous young westerners are seated in a circle of undersized plastic chairs. The still-flaming stick catches one of the party on the arm, leaving a scorch mark behind as it lands by her painted toes.

Keema sees the girl look down at the flaming baton, barely registering the pain as she watches it slowly fizzle out in the sand.

The older Thai man, maybe the boy's father, hurries over. He hands the balloon to the woman as if it were a band-aid.

Keema sees the girl's eyes light up and a grin spread across her face, the injury forgotten. The Thai man retreats, palms tight together against his chest, head bowed in an apologetic wai, while the indifferent westerner puts the balloon to her lips and, giggling, inhales the contents, to a scream of encouragement from her cohorts.

"Hey-hey. Drinks up!"

Ellie, nineteen and carefree, Keema's best friend since high-school, stands before her holding an oversized bucket of vodka and cranberry in her hand. Two curly fluorescent straws emerge from the bucket and Keema beams back at her.

Ellie, forever nineteen in Keema's memory, eager to partake in the global wake being held for the end of their future; an afterparty for the inevitable, already announced funeral of the planet.

Ellie, like Keema, determined to rinse every last drop from her youth while she still can, yet destined, as fate has it, never to witness the end of their world. Instead, she will bleed out on a pockmarked dirt road, one month later, trapped under the burning twisted shell of a motorbike. It is an accident that neither of them can foresee on a night like this, but one that will end their travels in tragedy and send Keema back to America in mourning and into a world of debt and depression. The pain of that moment, the lingering sorrow, will never truly lift until the day she feels her daughter - the little girl that she will name in Ellie's memory - shift in her belly for the very first time.

But that is the future. The near and the far. For now, Keema can only smile, drinking in all of the people, all of the unabashed life around her. All the young spirits full of possibilities never destined to occur. Young and carefree. Enjoying the last of the world's fruit before, in just a few short months, the announcements will come, the travel sanctions will begin, the world and its narrative will change forever and all of the innocence of this night will be washed away in the bloody hangover of dawn.

But that is another day.

For now, Keema takes her friend by the hand and, laughing, skips through the sand to a nearby table, absorbing all of the fading magic that the planet had seemed to possess on that night long ago, in a faraway place, once upon a time…

"Take a walk, Keema, let your brain unwind."

Keema hears the therapist's voice in her head as she stands in the gun-metal grey interior of the deserted corridor. Her bare feet sink into the plush blue carpet that lines the walkway. It's not quite the sands of a faraway-beach, but it will do for now.

"Just take your APD with you. We monitor the whole infant deck for irregularities. If Ellie wakes, you'll be notified. No need to worry. Take some Keema time."

Keema time.

She enjoys the phrase. Enjoys the night walks greatly.

In the daytime the corridors bustle with life, mothers moving here and there, the sounds of children on every corner, nurses pushing gurneys stacked with vitamin pods and nutri-boosters. A constant blur of colour and sound. A medley of movement and noise.

Not now.

Now Keema can take her time; wandering slowly along the empty labyrinthine corridors, with only the thrum of the ark to indicate that anything else on the ship is even moving.

She passes other doors as she walks. They click first to attention, then settle like soldiers at ease, as she winds her way around the immaculate steel structure, letting her hands trail against the cold metal, fingers tracing the glowing fractal patterns of partially disguised circuitry.

There are names on the doors, illuminated in immaculate fonts of radiant green light. Some of the names are familiar to Keema, others not so much. The lucky and the privileged. The arc is the great emancipator. Once on board there are no more class boundaries to adhere to. The old social standings are gone now. They are simply

mothers and their children. Divorced from their history. An anonymous brood with a future to fulfil.

As the rolling corridor diverges in a T-junction, Keema approaches a wall-mounted viewscreen and stops to examine the display. A greenish-blue globe spins at one end of the read-out and a tiny trail of electric arrows blinks out from it, marking the waypoint to their destination; the place where everything can begin again. Keema wonders what will happen when they get there. Will the friendly faces that coo to Ellie as she takes her out in the stroller once again turn up their noses and look down at her in the way that they would have done just a few short years ago; Before all this. Before the lottery.

Each night Keema passes the display, wondering if she will see something different on the screen; some measurable progress unfolding. Yet, so far, the display has barely moved. Only the numbers change. The vast impossible numbers that signify only the mystery of an unfathomable advance.

Keema is glad. She is not in a rush to rediscover her anointed place in the new world. For now, the limbo of the ark is its own special kind of heaven. She can remember, all too well, the hell that would have been her alternative.

Keema, twenty-five and at the end of her rope, stares into the bathroom mirror and weeps. In her hand, the two pink lines glare back at her from the pregnancy test. She lets it fall, in despair, to the cracked and blackened tiles of the floor.

From outside the apartment, she can hear the sirens wailing as the city burns in protest. From some distant alley an engine backfires and she jumps, thinking it a gunshot. From the apartment above her, the dull throb of techno that has slowly drained her of sleep and sanity continues, unabated.

This is surely the end.

Wrapped in her dressing gown. She stumbles into the filthy living room, a place she has long since given up on cleaning. Ignoring the roaches that scurry back across the torn linoleum floor, taking shelter under a pile of discarded takeaway containers, she collapses, sobbing onto the wreck of her sofa.

As if prompted, the screen crackles into life against the far wall, and a sharp looking news anchor begins covering the ongoing riots from the luxury of his polished studio. The image cuts to a burned-out cafeteria and a scene of armed police charging at a mob. Keema blinks away tears, watching the manic tickertape as it streams across the bottom of the picture, catching only key words from the headlines as they appear.

"President condemns…sympathy offered to family of UK leader killed in…. further bombings across west-coast…. looters move in on downtown…. Police officially withdraw…. military poised to intervene in…Exciting new lottery announced to…."

"Cindy," Keema sniffles, addressing the apartment AI, "Can you play good news?"

The screen dissolves in a blip of static and, when the picture returns, a smiling man is staring back at her from behind an oak panelled podium.

"My name is Roger Nemeth." says the smiling man. "and It is my pleasure to introduce to you to what we at NemCorp are calling: The Lottery of the New Frontier."

#

Botanical Gardens - > 5 minutes

Keema follows the sign. Keema has always followed the signs.

The trip to Thailand, as a fresh college-dropout, had, itself, been the result of a sign. Not a literal sign, in this case, but an ad she'd stumbled upon while procrastinating over a chemistry paper that she was destined never to turn in. The motorcycle accident had also been a sign. A sign that it was time to give-up and surrender willingly to the downward spiral and general negative vibe of the planet, finding her true calling as a member of the American underclass doomed to be left behind by the rich.

She hadn't expected further signs after that. Had almost stopped looking for them.

That's when he'd appeared. The Jesus of Silicon Valley, holding out an olive branch from the TV set while she had languished in the absolute nadir of her despair. Offering salvation, in the way that only a messiah can.

It had some flashy corporate name, of course, but the ordinary people had another name for it: The Last Chance Lottery.

Most people saw it for what it was; a distraction for the poor, something to keep them hoping while the rich fled the scene of the crime, taking the planet's remaining resources with them. It was an aspirin prescribed for a severed limb but it offered something, even a tiny fraction, of the one thing that had been utterly absent since the announcement.

It offered hope.

Hope for Keema, but also for the baby growing inside her.

It was a sign.

And somewhere, a small part of her had still believed.

"I'm Sorry Ma'am but you can't use food stamps to purchase lottery tickets."

Keema, twenty-five and pregnant, cannot make-out the furious response of the inebriated woman in front of her, only the clean, clear as day tone of the checking clerk.

"It's been that way since launch Ma'am."

Keema, one hand on her growing belly, winces as a further torrent of abuse is hurled at the clerk.

"What new rule would that be ma'am?"

She turns away, foot tapping, her bladder full to bursting. She wants only to buy the damned ticket and make it home. Thankfully, having heard enough, the disgruntled bag lady throws up her hands and hauls herself out of the way, cursing the uptight clerk on the way out of the door.

Keema steps forward and hands the grubby five-dollar bill to the clerk, a sour faced middle aged lady who looks Keema up and down with barely registered disgust.

"One ticket, please." Keema mumbles.

The clerk rolls her eyes. "Ma'am, maybe you oughta consider spending some money on food and think of that baby you got comin', 'steada wastin' money on fairy tales."

Keema blinks at the clerk. "I'm…sorry?"

The clerk is unrepentant. "I'm talkin' straight here, sister! Folk like you and me. You really think they gonna let us win? Them rich folk don't want us takin up a place on one of their spaceships. They'd rather give it to their buddies. This lottery is a joke. It's just a way to quell the riotin'. Everyone knows we-"

"I said one ticket, please!" Keema doesn't expect it to come out so forcefully and the clerk visibly flinches in response. Then she shakes her head, as if dismissing Keema's tone as the temper tantrum of a child. Punching in the code she hands over the ticket and the change. "You have a good day, Ma'am." The clerk sneers.

Keema turns, ticket in hand and exits the convenience store without looking back.

Welcome to the Botanical Gardens.

Keema smiles. Not just at the sign but at the sudden explosion of greenery. It is a jolt to her senses, as she finally exits the silvery grey monotony of the service corridors and steps into the unparalleled beauty of her favorite place on the ark.

Her bare feet sink into the woodchip lined gravel path. The pain is minor, but it's sharpness, its urgency are stark reminders that all is not lost, that she can still feel something of the world she left behind. She walks slowly, crunching along the winding path letting her gaze drift up through the lush green canopy of the installations to the smooth hexagonal transparency of the dome's structure and the infinite cosmos that stretches out beyond it. In the distance she can see the other arks, floating, like magnificently sea-sculpted pieces of driftwood. Lost in the emptiness of space that surrounds them on their journey. Her lungs pull in huge wafts of pine scented air as a pair of yellow winged butterflies flutter past her, disappearing into the nearby shrubbery, and the sound of a babbling brook fills the air.

In the daytime, Keema likes to bring Ellie here in the stroller. She nods and smiles dutifully at the other mothers she meets on her daily route. Yet it is at night, when few are still awake, that she can truly enjoy the peacefulness of this place. Her own private garden of Eden.

Finding her way to a nearby bench, Keema sits down, let's her toes dig into the gravel and begins the exercise her therapist has suggested. Focussing on that moment, that one moment of change that still lingers in her mind as a doubt.

Do I really deserve to be here?

She closes her eyes and imagines herself back in the roach infested apartment, with the TV chattering in the background. She remembers how she watched the numbers roll slowly in, that evening, eyes dancing back from the screen to the tiny ticket she held in her shaking hands. She mouths each number as it appears in her memory; a sacred, holy chant. She can still visualise the carton of orange chicken tumbling from her lap as the last number comes in and the realisation pours over her that all signs have led her to this moment.

She has won.

They can leave.

In her mind she pictures the smiling face of the TV Jesus extending his arms, only for it to slowly morph, as it always does, into the sneer of the convenience store clerk.

"Folk like you and me? You really think they gonna let us win?"

Keema concentrates. Imagines a ball of light engulfing the memory, trapping it, sealing it forever. Then she opens her eyes into the blackness of space that the bench overlooks and casts the memory out, seeing it slowly penetrate the transparent shell of the viewing deck, watching it sail out past the nearby arks, until it is merely another tiny dot of light, a distant star on an invisible horizon.

She sits quietly for a while after, wondering if, this time, she has really dispelled the anxiety for good. After a time, she feels a presence by her side and, a moment later, looks up to see the gentle eyes of the silver haired lady looking down at her.

"Hello dear. Can't sleep?" It is a kind voice with an unusual accent that Keema can't quite place. "May I sit with you?"

Keema nods.

The woman lowers herself slowly down onto the bench and Keema sees that she is holding a book in her hands. Its cover is lined with quilted green scales and a familiar pair of googly yellow eyes peek out from it.

The woman, still smiling, stares ahead, out of the viewing window and into the void of space and, for a second, Keema wonders if this lady can visualise all that she just sent out there.

"It's that one I think." says the silver haired woman, at last, pointing an index finger straight ahead.

"I'm sorry?"

"The Earth." smiles the woman, turning to meet Keema's eyes directly. "It's that bright one over on the right. So tiny now. Hard to think we've come so far already."

"Oh…I see. Yes." says Keema.

The woman turns back to the window and her previously benign expression seems to sink a little.

"I left my folks behind." she says. It sounds like a confession. "They sold the house to get us the ticket. I wonder…" she breaks off, seemingly unable to continue.

"I'm sorry." says Keema.

The woman sniffles, she seems grateful for the sympathy. "How about you?" she asks.

Keema takes a deep breath. There is no sense in lying anymore. It will come out eventually.

"I…I won the Last Chance Lottery." Keema confesses, speaking the words aloud for perhaps the first time, unable to reconcile why she needs to express remorse. "I was lucky." she adds.

Her companion seems initially startled, then she recovers her composure and pats Keema on the arm.

"Oh…well…that's wonderful, dear. You're both safe now, that's all that matters. Did you…did you leave anyone behind?"

Keema looks out into the starfield, focusses on the bright one just to the right. For a second, she thinks she sees it glow, like the fires of a burning baton in the white Koh Pha Ngan sand. Like the sheen of a mangled motorbike on a forgotten backwater dirt road. Like the flame of a rag stuffed into a bottle of kerosene as it arcs through the air toward the rushing mass of riot police. Like the gleam in her friend's eye as they run hand in hand through the balmy South East Asian night.

"Yes." she says, at last. Answering the question with finality. "I think we all did."

Her companion smiles sadly in understanding and opens the book on her lap.

"I know these are meant for the little ones," the woman says "but sometimes I come out here at night and read them to myself. I get comfort from these stories, you know? They all end the right way, if you know what I mean."

She turns back to the starfield in front of them and the mass of alternate arks making their lonely progress through infinity.

"And they all lived happily ever after." She says quietly. Then she turns to Keema with something akin to fear in her eyes. "Do you think…do you think they will?"

Keema continues staring out into the darkness.

"They all lived…" she repeats.

Try as she might to summon them, no further words will come.

⬥

Michael Teasdale is an English author living in Cluj-Napoca, Romania. His stories have appeared in Shoreline of Infinity, Litro, Novel Magazine and The Periodical, Forlorn. He can also be found in anthologies by Havok Publishing, World Weaver Press and Tyche Books with audio adaptations via 'Havok Story Podcast' and 'The Other Stories'. He can be followed on Twitter @MTeasdalewriter

The Mirror Girl

Isabel Hinchliff

We swim together, in the cloning vats beneath the city. Sloshing around in metallic liquid like otters, skin slick with the cloying, oily substance. My gun slipped out of my hand when she pushed me in, but I can still feel the sharp corners of the trigger pressing against the pad of my index finger like an iron-scented ghost, hungry for blood.

My vision is hazy. Sticky, reflective liquid drips from my eyelashes. She splashes nearby, flailing, desperate now. My clone.

She was supposed to just be target practice. I do that sometimes, when I need a reminder of what I'm up against—stand before the mirror, raise my gun, and shoot my reflection the minute it starts to move. I like to watch the bullet ripple-slide into the reflective metal, and I like to watch the newly-spawned clones fall as the steel lodges in their skulls. Like marionettes with their strings cut.

But some of them take longer to die.

I crouch in liquid metal, silent, senses spread, closing in. I can hear her, lacquered fingernails tapping dully against background splash-static. She's speaking, in a language older and more nuanced than simple morse code—a language of fast-blinking eyes and grandiose, open-handed slaps against the surface tension of the liquid. *Give me attention*, she cries, silently, with every movement of her body. *I'm being attacked, I'm innocent, I'm scared, help me, save me.*

Save me from the monsters.

I blink but the world refuses to resolve. A word slips through my mind, stirs the air like warm breath from smoky jaws.

My smoky jaws.

I smile, and metal seeps between my lips, bitter and cold. It sweeps around inside my mouth, smoothing out the sores and bumps, coating my throat in alien numbness. As the dregs reach the back of my throat I reflexively swallow, feel metallic droplets roll down my esophagus like candle wax.

She's close enough, now. Finally within my grasp. I reach out, alligator-quick, grab my clone's arm in both hands, and press down into her skin to hold her through the oily film that covers us both. I can feel the outline of her bones, my bones. The fleshy matter has been altered, but it's all on top of the same skeleton.

I pull at her, dunking under, bubbles streaming towards the surface, losing air in my exertion. I feel her oil-slicked skin slide towards me and I redouble my efforts, flailing my left arm sideways in an attempt to catch the side of the vat. My knuckles scrape against concrete and I grab it, pull us both out slowly. She struggles all the way, but I am stronger.

I made her this way. Beautiful. And breakable.

As I turn with my clone in a headlock, I catch a movement in my peripheral vision and swing my head around. The child-clone growing in the vat next to ours dives before I can see her face, her long black hair vanishing beneath the surface.

I'm already dragging my clone backwards across the floor, searching for something sharp. I've strangled them before, even drowned one, but I prefer to use a weapon. Wringing a carbon copy of my own neck is not a sensation I want to get used to.

One of the lights has shattered, scattering sharp pieces of glass over the concrete—I must have shot it earlier.

I drag my clone over, slit her throat with a wickedly curved glass shard, and leave her to bleed out on the floor.

As I blink and paw at my eyes, trying to clear my vision, I catch another glimpse of the child-clone floating in the next vat over. Light brown eyes, peering out at me beneath a thin covering of silvery liquid.

They remind me of my father's eyes.

I crouch over the pool, staring at the clone girl who is staring at me. Everybody's clones are stored down here, every single person each of us would rather be, growing and waiting for the moment when we catch a glimpse of our reflection and wish we could be better—thinner, taller, smarter, healthier, happier. Up close, I see that this clone girl's eyes are actually a bit darker than my father's. Her skin is a coppery shade of light brown, and her hair is long and black and luxuriant. Her face is kinda fat and round, though she might grow out of that.

She's younger than me, which means that whoever spawned her is younger than me, a real toddler out in the surface world. A real toddler who will someday feel those delicate little hands closing around her neck.

Probably not for a while yet, though. It's a deep vat, made for someone fully-grown.

I've seen young clones before, though usually in various states of shaggy adolescence, and I've wondered if I should fire a stray bullet into their abdomens, save someone else the trouble. But most people don't realize, not like me. They just let their reflection reach out its arms and choke off their air, die still exulting over the silky curve of its skin, the healthy bounce in its step, the unshakeable confidence in its steady gaze.

The clones are not born killers. Nor do they suddenly develop a bloodthirsty instinct when they emerge from the vat at the appropriate time, when the city's predictive algorithm cuts their life cycle short. No, they become killers after the city guides them to the right reflective object, when they catch their first glimpse of our deficient, desperate bodies. It is not murder, then, when they launch themselves at us tooth and claw. You can only be one person at once, after all. They are simply asking: who will you be?

I wonder who this little girl will be. Who she will kill and replace, as all clones do. You'd think it would be hell out there, people running haywire, all mirrors destroyed, but it's a peaceful process really. Every once in a while people look in the mirror and they become different. Sometimes it's obvious—some aspect of their faces, their height, their width—but sometimes it's more subtle, some aspect of their behavior. Some people look into the mirror and become kinder, smarter; others look into it and become more disrespectful, forgetful, reckless. As far as I can tell, there's no limit to how many changes any individual clone can have, just as there is no limit to how many times you can be cloned.

I would know. I've lost track of the number of clones I've killed.

I sigh, sit on the side of the vat, and dip my feet beneath the surface a few feet away from the clone girl. I stepped on some of the broken glass earlier, and I feel the vat's metallic liquid soak into the scratches. Those will dry hard, adding yet more strands of metal to the disorganized tapestry of scars webbing my feet, glinting in the light.

I am a patchwork girl, now, but at least I'm still alive.

Beneath me, the clone girl sinks a little, staring at my toes. She swims over, twisting her body in a kind of porpoise motion, and pokes at my instep tentatively, like prodding the sharp-toothed jaws of a now-lifeless beast.

I smile, watching her. It would be so easy, I think, to grab her under the shoulders and haul her, dripping with growth medium, back through the mirror and into my apartment.

Would she try to kill me?

Probably not. She's not *my* clone, after all.

I kick my feet gently back and forth in the liquid and watch the little girl follow my toes with her eyes. I'm so sick and tired of it all—the running, the fighting, the *knowing* that every time I even catch the barest glimpse of myself I'll have to kill some artificially-spawned copy made to be everything I wish I was.

It's so hard, staying human. A full-time job.

I snort, aloud this time. The girl in the liquid below me jumps back in surprise and tips her whole body so she's floating just beneath the surface on her back, staring up at me again with those huge, haunting eyes.

I put my hands over my face and promise myself that I'm living the life he wanted me to. He—

Something touches the back of my hands. Something wet, and oily.

I whip my hands back to see the girl splashing back into the pool of growth medium, wiggling her tiny fingers in front of her face, staring at them as if fascinated by how they work. A few air bubbles stream out of her slack mouth. She touches her fingertips together, sinking deeper. Then she opens her mouth, and I can see her trying to breathe in the metallic liquid, her ribs moving in fits and starts. She hits the bottom of the vat on her back, mouth open, body rigid. She stretches her hands out towards me, and I watch her eyes start to close, like a cat falling asleep, lazy and slow.

I stop thinking and just move. I slip into the vat, catch the girl under her arms, and push off with my feet, shooting towards the surface.

I sit her on the side of the pool and watch as she coughs up growth medium, leaving small splatters of metallic liquid on the concrete.

How the hell was she dying in there? She's clearly not grown up yet—this vat is made for an adult, and a sizable one at that. I must have disrupted the growth process somehow. Guess that's what happens when you dip your feet in things.

I suppress another snort, since the last one was so devastating.

The girl is done coughing now. She lies down amid the puddles of liquid metal, still breathing raspily.

I pull myself out of the pool, keeping my eyes on the girl. I touch her and her skin is cold, so cold it must be numb.

I walk a few steps away and try to visualize my way out of the cloning facility, focusing on the view through my mirror back home. I figured this out a few years ago; turns out if you're stuck down here and start wishing you'd never walked through the mirror—that you're back in your storage closet with that light-sucking rectangle placed firmly behind you—a silvery mass in the shape of a full-length mirror will suddenly appear before you. I know, it terrified me the first time too. But all you have to do is walk through it (it doesn't even feel like anything, it's not sticky or wet, purely a visual phenomena) to be back home in an instant. Not sure how the city gets that to work but I do know why it has this system—this must be how the clones get into our houses in the first place. They have all our memories and they wish they were back home. Simple, really.

The clone girl doesn't matter. Maybe she'll die, or maybe she'll roll back into the vat and the city will continue the growth process. Or…

I whirl around. Does she have her memories yet? Could she still visualize her way into someone's house, even though she can barely walk?

I force myself to take a deep breath. She's still lying there, motionless, on her side, breathing. Maybe she doesn't have a home yet, or maybe she's just too young or too weak to imagine one. Either way, it works.

I should leave now.

Instead, I just watch her lying there in the pool of growth medium, like a painting. I wonder if I'll have to take the long way up through the maintenance shafts, today; the adrenaline has worn off and my mind feels fuzzy inside, dense. I need to get more sleep.

At its edge, the pool of silvery liquid around the clone girl hits the puddle of blood around my now-dead clone. The two substances do not mix, but little bubbles of reflective silver invade the dull red, like oil in water.

I wonder if she's still breathing.

Something aches beneath my ribs, and I am also cold, covered in growth medium, and shivering.

I walk over, drop to my knees in the liquid, and roll the clone girl onto my lap. I press her to my chest, and feel her slippery arms clamp tight around my middle.

I'll kill her later.

I carry her back through the mirror and into my apartment. She's heavier than I expected. The metal-filled scratches on my feet tap against the concrete and then brush against carpeted floor.

We emerge into the broom closet by the kitchen table, where I store my mirror—the only reflective surface in my apartment, necessary to visualize my way out of the cloning vats. I shut the closet door firmly behind us.

First thing, I plunge us both into a shower, wiping off the metallic liquid with dish soap.

The girl seems tired. She warms up in the shower, but barely moves, clinging to me to stay upright after I place her on the floor. Free of growth medium, her skin is new and smooth, her lips red and unmarred by compulsive biting, her nails curved and clear and perfect. Not a thread of metal on her.

If only it could last. But maybe I can save her from some of my scars.

We steam a little in the winter air. I turn on the heater, change into some loose-fitting clothes, and find a big shirt for the little girl. It puddles around her feet, drags across the floor like a monarch's train. I wish I could take her back to those simpler times, when the collective interests of humanity were represented by mere *people*, powerful but ultimately contained, trapped within their own flesh.

I lead her over to the heater and sit against the wall, pulling her into my lap. With my foot, I reach for the towel we both used after our shower, now discarded on the floor by the closet. One of my metal toenails catches in the fabric, and I tug it over easily. I rub her hair vigorously with the towel, waiting for her shivering to subside.

My mother used to rub my hair like this, when I ran from the shower in a panic, screaming about the reflections in the faucet, the showerhead, the towel rail. We'd removed the mirror years ago, after I smashed it. After Dad died.

"It tried to take me, Ma," I would sniffle, as she caught my hair in her towel-wrapped hands.

"It's only the city, Gracie," she would say softly, tugging gently, rhythmically, at my hair. "Don't worry about it. It's just trying to make you feel better. All of us get cloned, every once in a while. It's normal."

Even then, I knew she was wrong about that. I didn't get cloned 'every once in a while,' I got cloned every single day, in every reflective surface I saw. I spawned clones in windows, in car doors, in overly large wedding rings. But I fought them. I fought them or ran from them.

I used to have friends, people like me who fought. We met in a basement, played music, exchanged stories. But the city got them all in the end. Perhaps I am the only one left in the whole world, who still has metal scars.

I won't let them win. I won't ever let them win. If I can't stop myself from wishing I was someone else, I can at least stop myself from *becoming* someone else.

I shake my head, breaking myself out of the reverie. The little girl's hair is dry now, warm from friction, even getting a little staticky. Her t-shirt is still wet, though, so I tug her over to the closet and slide her into another one, an old tye-dye that used to cinch just beneath my breasts. I'd liked it because it highlighted my waist without revealing the rolls of fat beneath.

On her, it cinches at the hips, making a little poofy dress. I carry her downstairs and collapse on the sofa, putting the girl down next to me. I start to turn her around to get a good look at her, but she makes that squeaky noise again and burrows into me sideways, pillowing her head on my stomach.

Ah well, I can imagine her, warm skin wrapped in faded greens and blues, silky black hair stretching to her waist.

A sea queen. Fitting, considering she's straight from the primordial ooze.

With her little head pressed against my ribs, I try to breathe slowly and deeply, pondering the immediate future. Her hair tumbles down my hip, a tangled mess. I'll have to brush that. My hair is short and frizzy—I barely even bother to comb it, these days. Do I have a brush buried in a drawer somewhere, from an old roommate or something? I used to brush my younger sister's hair, before it became so perfect and plasticky that brushing didn't even matter anymore.

Now that I think about it, I've probably had dozens of clone sisters. I should be a pro at this.

I look down at the girl again, her tiny hands pressed under her chin, tangled in strands of hair. I feel her weight against my stomach, her elbows digging gently into… my womb. She's young enough to be my daughter.

Maybe I'm getting soft in my old age, craving comforts I can never have while I'm still constantly running from myself.

As if to remind me, the girl shifts her arm slightly and the point of her elbow slides over one of my oldest wounds—a long scar of metal stretching from near my belly button to the top of my hip. The touch, the warmth, this feeling…

I know what safe and comforting feels like. Safe and comforting is cold steel against my palm and legs pumping strong to the rhythm of my breath. Safe and comforting is that first glimpse of my clone's eyes—wide, innocent, haunted, brimming with tears—that first glimpse when I know I can carve her beautiful face to pieces and dash those pretty eyes against the floor and feel them pop beneath the heels of my boots.

This feeling is… older.

The clone girl slowly curls her hand around my index finger, seemingly in her sleep. I'm tired, so tired, but I try to finish the thought.

Older… and more….

I let my eyes fall closed.

I'm dreaming of the time I found my Dad watching a scary movie. I'm about the same size as the little girl. The sea queen. Maybe just a little bigger. It's dark, and I can't sleep, so I pad downstairs to my parents' room in my socked feet to curl up in Dad's safe smell, as I have done on many other nights.

I think that I know what will happen, what will always happen. I will curl up in bed next to Dad and sink slowly into a dreamless sleep. He will wake up before Mom, for work, and carry me back to my bed in the gray dawn. I'll wake up in my own bed with a trace of his warmth and hazy memories of blundering around the house in the dark. If I mention it at dinner, Dad will put on his thinking face and ask me why I think I have such ominous dreams. And then wink.

Over many such nights, I will grow to love that word. Ominous. Ominominous. Onimonimonimous. Almost as good as "sea anemone" for lurking in your mouth, sliding and hiding between your teeth. A slippery word. The trout that was tickled, wove appreciatively between your fingers, and then slipped free as you closed them. That was my dream. To be onimonimonimous.

I had no idea what it actually meant of course.

But if I did, I might have used that word to describe how it feels as I pad up to the door of my parents' room and see artificial light seeping through the crack. Dad sits cross-legged on his side of the bed, headphones on, his laptop screen facing the door so the light won't wake Mom on the other side of the bed.

I stop just outside and watch the screen, entranced.

There's a gray forest, skeletal trees wreathed in smoke. The smoke swirls and dances, seeming almost to make pictures. I watch it form into the outline of a big toothy mouth, and then snap shut, dissolving just before the teeth close together. I giggle in half-amusement, half-relief.

Silly big toothy mouth, it's made of smoke and can't bite anything at all. I imagine trying to brush its teeth, trying to catch all the squirmy germy-worms.

I'm very good at catching the squirmy germy-worms. The dentist tells me so. And then she gives me a squidgy toy so I'll shut up while she talks to Dad about boring adult stuff.

The idea of a sparkly clean toothbrush bumping about in that gloomy gray forest makes me giggle even more, but Dad doesn't react. He just sits there, bent over his laptop in his headphones.

My giggles vanish into screams as a hideous white face pops up in the center of the screen, pale as ashes with blood-red lips and blue eyes that burn like coals, snarling so loudly that even I can hear it through Dad's headphones. Dad flinches, not at the face and the sound but at the slightly delayed beginning of my screams, and he slams the laptop screen down and turns around, but I am running, running…

Hands clamp down atop my shoulders, large and warm, and I stop moving. Dad spins me around and presses me against him, kneeling in the middle of the hallway. His cheek against my forehead is wet, but his breathing is even.

His voice is barely more than a whisper. "I'm sorry, I didn't mean to scare you."

My voice is raw, high, laced with tears. "There was a monster, Daddy, there was a monster and I thought it was going to eat me…"

He draws back, stares steady into my eyes. His eyes are kind of like the sea queen's, and dry, now.

"I'll never let any monsters eat you. I'll always keep you safe."

Of course he will. Of course I will always be safe, here in my father's arms. I smile against his shoulder.

"Good. That monster didn't look at all like he brushed his teeth."

Dad gives me a weird look as he stands up, shaking his head. Then a sudden smile creases his face. "If only he had you around, huh? You would catch all of those squirmy germy-worms right away." His voice is quieter than before.

"Exactly!" I proclaim, and he shushes me, but the noise seems to come from a distance, as my vision zooms out.

Ah right. This is a dream. I am older now, and this moment is drenched in nostalgia and that niggling voice of doubt: Was this the beginning, right here, right now? The beginning of the end for all of us?

In the dream, I can see my own eyes, brown like my father's, staring faithfully up at him. I can see my parent's room and the hallway, and my mother sitting up in bed, listening. Her eyes are fixed contemplatively on the laptop, but she smiles with us, when she hears Dad talking about the squirmy germy-worms.

"Don't wake up Mom," Dad whispers in the hallway, coming closer, and Mom scoops up the laptop and deposits it on the bedside table, lays down on her side with the covers bunched up around her shoulders, and slows her breathing. She stares into the dark while Dad brings me into the bedroom, tucks me under the covers, curls up around me. I watch our faces slacken and slip into sleep as my vision zooms out still further, and I'm surfacing, going up but not far enough, still, stuck, in the dream, the memory, the dream…

A few weeks later, I get cloned for the first time.

I look in the mirror at my fat red little cheeks and think of my porcelain dolls, about how pretty they are. About how Mom picks them up, carefully, with both hands, and smiles at their smiles, painted and perfect, not all jagged and scrunchy and wide like mine. In the mirror, the color drains from my face, my eyes light up with freaky electric-blue, and my lips paint over with bright, bright red. It was the same face that lived in the gloomy gray forest, but this time it had little pudgy arms with grasping fingers, and they closed over my wrist and pressed against my bones and pulled, just like…

Just like I did, today, with the clone I killed this morning. Just like I held on to her in the depths of the vat, trying to break through her slippery metal skin and affix my bones to hers, so I could drag her thrashing from the pool and sink in my metal teeth, victorious, to squeeze between my bare hands the lifeblood of the ominominominous…

I wake up, breathing hard, to find the clone girl shifting in her sleep. Her tummy rumbles, low and loud. She shifts again, puts her hands just beneath her ribs, curls around them.

I pick up the girl, balancing her on my hip, and make my way over to the kitchen. She grabs onto my shoulder, pulling me off balance a little, and I pause for a second to rearrange her arms so she's hugging me across my middle. She clamps on tight.

Little limpet.

I survey the fridge. I have minced meat and rice left over from my weekend prep, but I'm worried that'll be too spicy for her. What do little girls like?

Pasta. Butterfly pasta, sticky with cheese. That was always my sister's favorite. That is, until the mirror took her and came back with what I called the "health freak" clone. That creature wouldn't eat pasta anymore because it wasn't good for her "figure".

I wonder, briefly, if she would have liked lentil pasta. Or edamame. They do have a lot less calories, usually.

Maybe I should have tried to get to know her better.

Anyway.

I move closer to the cupboard so I can rifle in the back with one hand. Beans, salsa… I do have cheese in the fridge. I bought some last week, but I never got round to making lasagna with it.

Next to my ear, the girl makes a happy noise, some sort of squeal, but with her mouth open so it almost sounds like words.

She's reached her right hand into the cupboard and is patting a cardboard packet gently, like it's a good dog or something. To humor her, I pull it out to take a look. "Italian Farfalle," I read disbelievingly, probably botching the pronunciation.

Butterfly pasta.

I dump the pasta into a pot, fill it with water, and set it on the stove. The girl cuddles against my side and watches.

While the water begins to boil I just stand there, trying not to think. Trying not to think about my sister, about my mother, about how far away they all are, how many times the mirrors have taken them and spat another person back out, someone unrecognizable. Trying to just live here, in this moment, and watch the bubbles form.

I turn, a bowl in each hand, towards my wobbly square of a kitchen table (it's the table that's wobbly, not my hands, and definitely not my legs), and there is the clone girl, standing on a chair. Her tiny hands are braced over the top of the table, and I realize that she's trying to climb up onto it. Which doesn't look like a good idea, because the table is an awful lot taller than her, and how on earth did she even get up onto the chair anyway?

I rush over, dump the steaming bowls on the table, and grab her by the middle while she squirms. I manage to maneuver her onto my hip again, but she starts crying suddenly, and I realize that a few strands of hair have got tangled in the back slats of the chair, so I carefully wind them free, muttering about how I need to find a reflection-free pair of scissors. I grab some cushions, stack them on the chair, and place her atop them.

There. A proper sea queen now, passing judgement on my cooking. Did I put enough cheese on it? Would it be better with some salt and pepper, perhaps, maybe some tomato sauce?

She launches herself facefirst into the bowl of pasta and begins slurping it up.

I start laughing. Between fits of giggles, I manage to find a piece of paper towel, clean her up, and start feeding her individual forkfuls in a much more dignified manner. She complains (in her open-mouthed, squeaky way) every time a mouthful doesn't have any cheese on it, so I have to sprinkle more cheese on each layer, until finally her bowl is empty.

My giggles stop cold as I remember that she's a clone and I was going to kill her.

Do I have to, though? She really seems like a normal little girl. Not that I know anything about normal little girls, but she definitely doesn't seem dangerous. Maybe just this once, I could let my guard down...

Maybe just this once, and then what about the next time, when one of my clones gets ahold of a knife somewhere and looks at me with that fierce, blazing desperation...

There's a creaking noise. A creak like the closet door opening.

I spin around, already feeling my heartbeat speed up.

The clone girl stands before the open closet door, staring into the mirror. The door opens outward away from the kitchen, so I can see the clone girl sideways against the open door—the sea queen, sideways on a background of white paint. I can't see her expression, but she shifts from foot to foot, swaying. What is she seeing in there? What is she wishing for?

I open a drawer and take out my backup gun—a pocket pistol, already loaded. I circle wide, trying to center myself, and then I step behind her, into the background of her reflection in the mirror. I scrutinize her reflection, trying to find the difference. Is the face a little narrower maybe? The eyes slightly brighter than usual? The hair, maybe it's... more wispy?

The girl raises a hand and waves at the mirror. Her reflection waves in sync. It doesn't reach out to grab her, pull her in. The clone girl giggles, scrunches up her face. So does her reflection. She runs up closer to the mirror, pressing her fingers against it. She does not fall through, does not pass through an insubstantial barrier to emerge into the mirror-world, the endless lines of concrete vats.

I know that this is possible, to look in the mirror and see nothing but your own reflection. It happens to people all the time, apparently. But it's never happened to me. Not that I can remember, anyway.

I realize that I'm crying. My throat makes a strangled noise.

The little girl turns from the mirror and runs toward me, talking again, in that strange open squeaky language I feel like I should know. I bend down to catch her, hold her. She is warm and smells like cheese.

I open my eyes over the clone girl's shoulder and see myself in the mirror.

In my reflection, I'm thinner, with larger breasts, and I bend down towards the clone, making eye contact, murmuring quietly. Then my reflection stands up and starts to walk towards me. I curl one arm around the clone girl, raise my other arm over her shoulder, and shoot my clone in the gut. She doubles over, falling to the floor, still inside the mirror.

The clone girl squeals when she hears the gunshot, burying her face against my shoulder.

"Don't worry," I murmur. "It's okay."

I shut the closet door.

I pick up the little girl and carry her to the sofa, placing her beside me. She turns to me, makes eye contact, and makes three noises in her strange open language.

"Wah Wah ah?" she says.

"Well," I say, and my voice croaks. I haven't actually spoken to someone in a long time. I clear my throat. "Well, it was a clone. It was my clone. Not yours. You didn't have a clone."

She just stares, with those eyes that remind me of my father's.

I cover my eyes.

She cuddles against me and makes more noises, nothing recognizable this time.

My father never wanted me to clone myself. The mirror-systems were new, back then, and he—

Fingers touch the back of my hands. The clone girl.

She folds my fingers down against my cheeks, carefully, one at a time, so she can see my eyes. She smiles.

"Hey, um…" I say to her, using words, which still feels strange. "Do you want to hear a story?"

She flops back on the sofa, still staring up at me.

"Are you sure?" I ask slowly, feeling my voice go lower, conspiratorial. Let me tell you a secret. Just between us girls. "It's a scaaary story."

She smiles at the way I say 'scary', with too much 'kuh' and a long 'eh' sound.

"Once upon a time, there was a little girl who was a lot like you, really."

I bop her on the nose and she looks a little annoyed, covering the bottom half of her face with her hands.

"And she looked in the mirror and saw… a monster." On 'monster', I raise my curled hands above my head like claws in a sudden movement, and the girl jumps back and makes a high-pitched noise. I start to reach my hands towards her neck, and I feel the ominominominous curled between my fingers, thick and sticky with memories of violence.

Maybe, this is when I kill her.

"The monster had bright blue eyes and cherry-red lips, and reached out its hands toward the little girl, but it didn't really have clawed fingers, it had lovely perfect little curved nails just like yours…"

I place my hands to either side of the little girl's neck and try to feel that steel-metal cold conviction that I feel when I look into my own eyes.

"…but she imagined that it had clawed fingers, so she screamed."

The little girl does not scream. She just stares, and I run my hands over her shoulders and down her arms to hug her around her middle. I draw her into my lap, and she starts giggling.

She squirms around to sit with her back against me, head resting just beneath my breasts.

I curl my right arm around her and I hold her tight while I act out the rest of the story one-handed against an invisible foe.

"And her father, like a knight in shining armor, came running, except he was in his bathrobe, with his hair all stickity-uppity and his glasses messed up, and the minute he saw the monster he picked it up by its pudgy little arm and dashed its head on the bathroom floor.

"And so, the monster was vanquished."

This isn't the end of the story. The story ends with another clone, and another, and another after that one, and my father wading into the mirror to kill them all. Until the day he never came back.

But she doesn't need to know that bit.

The clone girl has slid down my lap and fallen asleep. Her hair is tangled again, beneath her head, so I tug it out and stroke it straight.

My perfect little girl, who looked in the mirror and saw nothing but herself. No expectations. Nothing she would rather be.

Yes. I would be sad if she lost that.

I will be sad when she loses that.

My tears fall into her hair. They don't wake her.

In the morning, I wake up to find the little girl staring at me. She's standing up on my lap, and I can see myself reflected in her wide pupils. In my reflection, the metal scars are gone from my face. There are new lines across my forehead and next to my eyes, faint, not quite wrinkles yet.

I feel different. My eyes are wide and shimmering, and my hands tremble. But I am stronger, now, than ever before.

I am still a person. I am still the same person.

I get up, and start thinking about breakfast.

⸺⟨◇⟩⸺

Isabel Hinchliff is a 4th year undergraduate student at the University of California, Berkeley. She is double majoring in English and Cognitive Science, with a minor in Creative Writing. She is a Managing Editor at Berkeley Fiction Review and a Submissions Editor at Uncanny Magazine. Her writing has been previously published in Elegant Literature. In her free time, she cooks gluten-free food, writes dark speculative fiction, and teaches English. You can find pictures of her cats on Twitter @IsabelHinchliff.

The Price of Green

Jonathon Mast

"I heard you had green." A gray patched coat clings to his gaunt frame. The ashfall had coated his shoulders. Hollow eyes plead with me to let him in.

It could all be faked. The barons hire a lot of people these days.

"You're crazy," I say. I try to shut the door on him.

"Please," he says, quick as a gull after a morsel. "Please. I've never seen green." He's trying to be quiet, but the gears have deafened him. Like they deafen everyone else in the city.

And he's telling the truth. Means he doesn't work direct for a baron, or else he would have seen green before.

"What's your name?" I ask through the crack in the door.

He wraps his coat tighter around himself. "James," he says. He tries to smile but coughs instead.

Another truth. His name really is James. Doesn't help me much, though. There are more men with that name in the city than there are orphans. I need something more specific.

"There's a price," I tell him.

"I'll pay." He proffers two iron coins in a gloved hand.

I recoil. "Put them away. I don't want that." I don't need that. I need something else entirely. "You ever sing?"

He shakes his head.

"Liar."

His eyes widen in surprise. He stammers. He looks around the city street. The cobbles. The mostly-empty husks of buildings in this part of town.

Ever since the winds shifted and all the ash falls in these streets, people just don't want to live here. There are bums lying in the gutter here and there, hollow men who have forgotten how to speak. The clanging from the factories is near overpowering. A drunk stumbles nearby. A constable strolls across the field of my vision. He pays me no mind. James glances at the officer and looks away quickly.

"You sing," I prompt him.

"Only to my girls." He looks down, embarrassed.

"You have daughters."

"Yeah. Matilda and Gracie." The corner of his mouth twitches just a little.

"How many songs do you sing to them?"

He shrugs. "I know a few."

"Then. The price to see. You'll sing one of the songs you sing for them."

I see the war in his face. "You won't laugh," he says.

I answer with a laugh.

He takes a step backward. He's never heard a woman make a sound like this. Yes, probably from his daughters, who haven't learned how dark the city can be. But something so without guile? Something so unguarded? From a grown woman?

"I don't laugh at a song given." My smile is more genuine than anything he's ever experienced. "I laugh that it even needs to be asked. If I didn't laugh, I would weep, and my weeping would bring even worse things to this city. Come in, James. If you will sing." I open the door.

He enters, and I latch the door behind him. It would do no good for someone to enter now. Not when I am about to feed.

I lead the way down the corridor. A few doors line the dark hallway. They all lead into the ruins of apartments. People once lived here. After a few moments, we enter into a courtyard. And there, poking out from the drifts of ash, bathed in the diffuse gray light, is the weed. Just a thistle, really. Spiny leaves and a dull purple blossom. It's all that I can get to grow here.

He gasps. He rubs his eyes and stares. He blinks. It is so hard to absorb a color you've never seen before. Ash gathers on his shoulders, on his hair. His hands tremble. A tear gathers in the corner of his eye. "They say. They say that once this color reigned. That you could see it anywhere."

"Once," I answer. "And maybe again. Someday."

He swallows. "It's worth your price."

"Then sing."

And he does. His voice is rough from the smoke. He is untrained. Where I was grown, he would have been reduced to shadows for such a poor performance. Yet such offerings here are rare. So few parents remember how to sing for their children. Without green, there is no need for music. And without music, how could I nourish what green I can grow?

He sings a song about cats visiting the moon and chasing the mice that eat the cheese there. It's a silly little song that teaches nothing. It has no purpose other than to swaddle a child in the loving voice of their parents.

I savor every poor note, every cracked syllable, every half-interval. I drink it all in.

Finally, his voice falls silent. His eyes

have not left the weed. He blinks. "I should probably pay you. You said I should sing?"

I shake my head. "You have done enough."

He furrows his brow. "But I never paid."

"You have done enough," I repeat. He will never sing that song to his children again. The melody is gone. I have swallowed the words.

"It's so beautiful." His eyes continue to devour the sight of the weed.

"Remember it, then. Come back to me. Bring your children. They should see the color green." Oh, and to eat a child's mirth? That could sustain me for so, so long.

James hesitates, but finally turns away. He does not want me to see him weeping.

I accompany him back to the door. I let him out onto the street.

He turns to face me. "Thank you," he whispers.

"Bring me more song. Bring me more light. Perhaps I will be able to grow more green," I tell him.

James nods. "I would like that."

"So would I," I answer. "So would I."

"They should see it," he says. James stands in the ashfall, shivering. Two girls stand between him and the street. He glances around. He's a good father. He wants them safe.

The girls see me for what I am, though. The older one, nine summers old and her left hand already missing two fingers from the hungry gears, shivers. The younger one, five summers old, peers up at me. "Why are your eyes funny?" she asks.

James shushes her.

I laugh. It's my free laugh again. The girls instantly brighten to hear the sound. James still feels uncomfortable. I invite the three in. The girls want to explore all the rooms of the building. The younger one asks if there are ghosts. The older one peers through every door. James, though, knows the way and pushes them toward the courtyard.

He gasps when he sees it. "It's grown," he whispers.

"You fed me. When I am healthy, the weed is healthy," I say.

The girls approach and kneel near the weed. The older one reaches out to touch it ever so gently. "Why is it spiky?" she asks.

"To protect it from gears and anyone who would steal it away," I answer.

"Like the barons?"

"And others," I answer.

"Why aren't there more?" the younger one asks.

"Because the iron keeps us out," I answer.

"Us?"

I sigh. James assumed I was one of his kind, and why not? I appear like him. I may act strange, but so would anyone protecting something so precious. "Iron is poisonous to people like me. And to you, too, but not to your body. Have you heard your father sing?"

The girls look at each other and giggle.

"Have you heard anyone else sing?"

They look at each other again and search each other's faces. They ponder for a long time. Finally they turn back to me. "I heard a man on the street once," the older one says, "On my way to the grindery. It was sort of a fast thing, like one of the grinding gears. I liked it."

I nod. "The city needs to be powered, and not just by coal. It's powered by song and story and everything that makes you humans so wonderful. And if the city feeds on it, that means people like me can't be here anymore. Because, you see, I feed on such things, too. I'm starving. And without people like me, nothing green can grow."

And the younger girl springs to hug me. She already smells of iron. It coats her skin. I feel myself sizzle, my flesh rebelling against the touch even as I try to absorb her adoration.

I finally release her.

She gazes up into my face. "Can I sing?"

"I hope so."

And she sings. The song has no words, but it is full of joy that only a child can have. Her sister joins in. James stands back, his eyes full of wonder.

And then he sees the weed.

It is growing. Grass is poking up through the ash. Tears water my face.

"Yes, children. Like that," I whisper.

And when their voices fade, they shout in surprise and joy. "Look! It grew!"

Their father embraces them.

"Can we keep coming back to feed you?" the little girl asks.

"I would like that. Very much," I answer. "And if you do, bring more children. Perhaps, perhaps we will grow again, and green will return. But there is a price," I warn.

"What is it?"

I hesitate. "The city will eat up your songs and your stories, grinding it out between gears with a terrible hiss. You will be left hollow. But I will eat your joy just as surely."

The girls examine each other's faces.

James takes their hands. "I think it's time to go, girls." His words are rushed. Of course they are. A father protects his children.

"There is a price for seeing green," I tell him.

"You said I paid you already."

"There is more green now."

He looks back at the freshly-sprouted grass. "I cannot give you my children."

"This is the price. You will allow them the choice."

"No."

And I collapse. The price is not given.

James holds his little girls' hands. They are out in the street in the ashfall. "How did we get here?" he mumbles.

"Daddy. The pretty lady took us out here."

"What pretty lady?" he asks.

"The one who showed us green."

He shakes his head. "There's no green in the city, girls. Never has been. Come on. We need to get home or your mother will kill us."

I watch from the door. They do not see me. They will never see me again.

There is a price for green, and until it is paid, this city will never see it again.

Jonathon Mast lives in Kentucky, US, with his wife and an insanity of children. (A group of children is called an insanity. Trust us.) You can find him at https://jonathonmastauthor.com/

No Rescuers for an Aging Princess

Jo Miles

Once upon a time, a prince married a princess. Then the prince died. What was left?

For days, the question had wrapped her mind in a fog, a riddle with no answer. Or perhaps the riddle contained its own answer, and this was what remained: these endless days, this helpless spiraling around the same unrelenting question. This numbing fog was worse than any enchantment, for a magic curse would have its cure, and this had none.

A knock at the door tugged her back to herself. The maid paused in her too-cheerful chattering and admitted Rigel, her husband's seneschal.

No, her husband's no longer. Her son's, now.

"Are you settling in comfortably, Highness?" Rigel asked.

It was a dutiful question, holding no real interest in her comfort. She gazed out through the cheap, distorting window glass, down to the inn's courtyard where the men were unloading the wagons. Her son Bertrym must be among them, giving instructions with the careful air of nobility he cultivated as he strove to fill his father's absence, but the glass blurred her view, and she could not see him. A grown man now, Bertrym no longer needed his mother.

Rigel cleared his throat; she hadn't answered his question. "I won't disturb you, Highness. The journey from the capital is always taxing, and with the funeral, you must be doubly weary. I will have dinner brought up to your tomb."

No, no, no. *Room*, he'd said *room*, not tomb, no matter its plainness or narrowness. The slip jarred her, and she saw the preciseness of a hole in the ground, its corners perfectly and appallingly square as they lowered in Tremaine's frail body. Shouldn't graves be as messy and rough as death? Not this tidy room with four close walls…

No! No more living tombs. Enough.

"Thank you, Rigel, but I will dine downstairs tonight."

His brows rose. "Surely you'll be more comfortable here, Highness."

"Perhaps, but nevertheless, I will dine downstairs."

Rigel's lips pressed together. "I suppose there is no real harm. I'll invite your son to join us."

The dining room was crowded with people of every sort: merchants and soldiers, traveling families, passing heroes and local scoundrels. Their gazes pressed in on her as she took her seat, and fog gathered at the edge of her vision.

Bertrym exchanged low, sharp words with the seneschal, then hastened to join her. "Mother, are you well? I expected you would want to rest in your room, as is your custom."

Her son was as solicitous as his father, if with different reason. No young man stepping into his new role with his father's men would want his mother hovering over him. The corners of her mouth twitched, not quite achieving a smile.

"I've done nothing but rest and take refuge since your father died," she said. *And too much of it while he lived.*

The conversation in the room lapped at her awareness. Gossip made small splashes that spread like ripples on a clear lake.

"Prince Tremaine's widow."

"Really! Here?"

"Such a fine man…"

"What an unexpected privilege, Your Highness!" The man who joined their table uninvited wore a velvet doublet and heavy purse that marked him as a merchant of status. "Good man, your late husband. My sincerest condolences for your loss."

She could not look at him, so she bent her head over her soup. Pungent with onions, salty as tears. His death continued to pummel her at the least expected moments.

How she'd raged when her father had insisted she marry Tremaine! All she'd done was break the handsome young prince's enchantment. He'd tricked her into kissing him — really, he'd head-butted her with his mouth, an insistence that much, much later would become a joke between them. As if she would ever have kissed a goat! But curing an enchanted prince apparently necessitated marriage.

Her mother had assured her over and over that love would follow, as her mother had come to love her father. She'd raged at that promise, too.

But despite all her resistance, she *had* come to love Tremaine. People remembered her husband for his feats — for his battle of wits with the wizard

Kolyar where he won his magic horse Nightwind, or for scaling the Poxed Ogre's tower single-handedly to rescue his beautiful bride after her kidnapping. Fewer people remembered the warmth of Tremaine's smile, or his gentle teasing. They thought he was joking when he said she'd nearly charmed that ogre into releasing her before he arrived, but Tremaine always, sheepishly, spoke of the truth.

"My lady is still distraught over her royal husband's death," said Rigel. "Please, do not disturb her."

"Of course not," said their unwanted guest. "I only wanted to pay my respects, and perhaps hear about his heroism. What stories you all must have of his majesty!"

Rigel, on the verge of shooing him away, paused at the prospect of an audience, and seemed to deem the merchant acceptable company. "I won't trouble my lady with stories of Prince Tremaine, but I could tell you quite the tale about…"

Not my father, don't say my father. Nor my grandfathers, nor my uncles, nor my brother, don't make me talk about any of them…

"…About her father."

"Her father? You mean King Edward?" The merchant perked up in realization. "Ah! She's the princess who drank from that enchanted spring, isn't she? It turned her into a newt, I believe."

"A squirrel, wasn't it?" asked Bertrym. He leaned forward, eager for the story.

"No, it was a vixen," said Rigel with authority, while she stared at her hands. "The old king has told me many times how her brother the prince hunted tirelessly until he found and trapped her in fox form, and how the king himself forced the old witch who enchanted the spring to reveal the cure."

It hadn't been like that at all. Her brother had made her drink from the spring as a prank, and her father put the blame on that poor old woman — a hedgerow healer, not even a witch! — to spare the family's reputation. She'd been furious when she was restored to her true form, but by then, the story had spread.

"Ha! She's lucky her brother and father were there," said the merchant.

A young adventurer, listening from the next table, snorted. "Bet she won't go drinking from strange springs anymore."

The fog was closing in again, yet it could not shut out the names, the twisted stories, the knife-sharp flashes of memory. She gulped down her wine, willing the conversation to move on.

"Her brother, is that Prince Vonn? The one who…"

"Oh, yes!" cried Bertrym. "Tell the one about…"

She couldn't. Murmuring excuses about needing to rest, she rose from the table. Rigel and Bertrym glanced up with polite concern, but were too absorbed in their stories to worry much about her. As soon as they looked away, she slipped out the front door.

Outside, the stars shone from a black velvet sky. Beyond the pool of light around the doorway, the road dimmed to a ghostly ribbon. Half-dried mud sucked at her heels as she walked, probably ruining her shoes, but she couldn't trouble herself to care.

A signpost rose from the crossroads. Stepping close, she could just make out the names carved on its arms. South lay the capital, home of King Edward, once her home as well. A place too full of memories. To the west lay the port whence her uncle Roben set out across the sea and later returned with the egg of the wyvern that became his battle companion. To the north was the forest of Vall, where her brother passed the tests of a secretive wizard's order to win training in the magical arts. She wondered: would Vonn be a wizard today if not for the "accident" at the enchanted spring? She suspected not.

To the east… that way lay Tremaine's castle, which awaited Bertrym as its new ruler. A place she called home by habit, for lack of a better name. The place where she would live out her days, sitting in high towers and setting all her decisions in the hands of others. The thought made her bones scream.

She was the king's daughter, the wizard's sister, the adventurer's niece. She had been the hero's wife, and now the hero's widow. And soon, very soon, Bertrym would make legends of his own. She saw greatness already straining for expression within him. He would become a great leader and a legendary swordsman.

And then she would be the warrior's mother.

Greatness surrounded her on all sides, pressing in. She'd loved her husband, and she loved her son with a fierceness. No less did she love her father, or her brother, or any of these towering figures in her life. But between them, she felt herself pressed away to nothing. Rubbed and rubbed like a piece of soap until no sliver of her was left to call her own.

She flung her head skyward, gasping for breath. The cooling evening air filled her lungs, and she sucked it in, trying to draw down the cold calmness of the stars. They remained stubbornly fixed in the sky, and she remained alone.

A thud made her jump. A muffled curse floated from the direction of the stables, followed by a horse's whinny. That sounded like Nightwind! She knew the sound of her late husband's cherished stallion like she knew Tremaine's own voice. Nightwind never made a fuss without cause; the magic steed had better manners than most humans. Perhaps the grooms had neglected Rigel's instructions about Nightwind's care. She went to check on him.

The stable was dark, but not empty. Nightwind stomped in irritation, his ears forward, and the horses near him whickered and shuffled, infected by his unease. As she slid the door open, she thought she heard the rush of feet. A chill ran down her back.

Lighting a lamp revealed nothing amiss, nothing to explain Nightwind's behavior. She patted his neck. "There, loyal steed. What's upset you?"

His ears pivoted in warning, but she turned too slowly. A strong, slender hand clamped over her mouth, and cool metal pressed to her throat.

"Not a sound, y'hear? Silence!" The voice sounded gruff, strained.

She nodded calmly, comforted by the old familiarity of the threat. *Kidnapping!*

And I thought I was past this sort of thing. At least I'll be part of one last story.

Except… there was no more Tremaine to rescue her. It would have to be her son this time, but Bertrym had never rescued a princess before, and she was no longer a fair maiden, and who had ever heard of a prince rescuing his *mother?*

How did this story go, then? Would rescue come for her at all? The thought rippled through her muscles like the magic of that enchanted spring, transforming her. She hadn't felt so alive since that day in her fox form, except maybe in the ogre's tower when escape was so nearly in her grasp. She'd never told Tremaine that when he'd appeared on the tower stairs, her first, fleeting reaction had been disappointment. Her rescue had left her with a question, unanswered all these years: could she have done it on her own?

And here before her was a new story, one she'd never been part of before, and she didn't know how it ended. That unknown terrified and thrilled her.

"I'll have to tie you up so you don't make trouble," her captor said in that gravelly voice. "If you behave, I won't hurt you. Got it?"

"I understand. But if you're after horses, I'd advise you not to take Nightwind."

"Nightwind?"

"The one you came for. The one with a coat blacker than the night sky, with stars in his eyes."

"How did you know—" The horse thief growled. "That horse is the whole point of this."

"I know, because of his magic. But that horse knows loyalty. He'll run away every chance he gets, and won't bear you willingly. You're not the first to attempt to steal him."

"Who are you, to know all this?"

"I'm no one," she said, and that was true enough. "But I know that horse. Don't take him."

The thief grunted and pulled her sideways toward the wall, probably searching for a rope. By the light of the fallen lamp, she caught a glimpse of the thief's face in profile: narrow chin, full lips. She gasped.

"You're a woman!"

"So?" the thief said.

"I'm just surprised."

"You think a woman can't steal horses?"

"I suppose I never thought about it."

Now that her identity was discovered, the thief's voice lost its forced depth, returning to a more natural pitch, though it remained biting. "Of course not. You're a noble lady. Here, sit."

She sat patiently while the thief tied her up. It wasn't well done — she knew what good, strong knots felt like — but it seemed to satisfy the thief, who moved on to Nightwind's stall and held out a handful of sugar lumps. Nightwind snorted in derision. When the thief pressed harder, he snapped at her fingers.

"Damn beast! Here, it's sugar! Why won't you like me?"

"He likes *me*," she said, "and you've just tied me up."

The thief rolled her eyes, but the widow blinked, stunned to silence by the idea that her own careless words had conjured in her head. An idea too absurd to contemplate, for she was a princess, widow of a hero, daughter of a king! It would be in no way appropriate for her to… no, she couldn't. She heard her father's disapproval, her brother's scorn, Tremaine's gentle chiding. It wasn't fitting.

For a long time she sat, watching the thief attempt to use sweets and a soft voice to charm a horse who knew every trick there ever was. The longer she sat, the more insistently the idea stirred within her, and the more her fog melted away. For the first time since her husband's death — perhaps for the first time in decades — her pent-up heart writhed, questing for its freedom.

"Come with me, damn you!"

The thief grabbed Nightwind by the chin, and he reared up at her. She scrambled away. The other horses stamped in response, and one whinnied in alarm. This horse thief didn't seem to know much about horses.

"What do you need Nightwind for?" the widow asked. "There are a dozen more amenable horses in this stable."

The thief drew back from the stall, eyes narrowed. The girl was thin, built of so many dangerous angles that the sword at her belt seemed superfluous, but the hardest edge was in her eyes. There was a story in those eyes.

"I need more than a plain old horse," the thief said. "I aim to make a name for myself."

"Oh?"

"Like I would tell *you*," she said, but her lips worked, and she seemed unable to keep from bragging. "What I can tell you is that I mean to steal more than horses. I'm headed to a place of dangers and wonders, full of treasures that the great lords suppose to be safe because no thief could ever find their way there. And most couldn't, but I reckon I could, if Nightwind would tolerate me riding him." She glanced at Nightwind, whose eyes rolled upward. "But that'll never happen, will it?"

She slumped to the dirt floor, scowling up at the horse.

"I don't know about that," said the widow, the oft-rescued princess, the royal mother whose days of purpose were gone before they began. She had never been more than a symbol in the stories of others, and Bertrym no longer needed her even for that. She could sit in her tower, alone and forgotten and purposeless, until the time came to follow Tremaine, or…

This is madness, she thought, *but how is it madder than the rest of my life? Because I'm choosing it? Maybe so.* She made her decision, and gripped it tight.

"He'd tolerate me."

"And a lot of good that does me!"

"It would, if you take me with you."

"Ha!" The thief threw her head back and laughed, until she noticed that the older woman wasn't smiling. "What, you're serious?"

"I may not look it, but I've had my share of hard travel and dangerous places." Another truth: she'd been part of enough other people's adventures. The more she spoke, the less mad the idea seemed, and the more she yearned for this thing she hadn't realized was missing. "I know how heroes do things. Take me with you."

The thief frowned. "Heroes don't

have partners. Neither do thieves."

"And women can't be either one. You're breaking the rules already."

"You want me to untie you so you can run away."

"I swear to you on my husband's grave, I do not. Please, take me."

"Why?"

"Nightwind won't cooperate unless you bring me."

"I mean, why do you want this?"

That gave her pause. She had to convince the young woman that this tug on her heart was real, and that she wouldn't regret this decision come tomorrow. She had to believe that, yes, she could have escaped the ogre on her own, and that everything would have been different if she had.

Outside stood the crossroads, one arm pointing toward a home she'd long since left behind, another pointing to a home where she would sit and rot until she died. But the other arms, those pointed to places she'd never seen.

"I want adventures that no one will try to rescue me from. I want trouble of my own choosing. You said you wanted to make a name for yourself. I want that, too."

The young thief stared. "Who *are* you?"

"I don't know. My whole life, I've never known, and I want to find out."

Rigel and Bertrym were sitting in the tavern, hoping Tremaine's widow would keep to herself if they thought of her at all. Bertrym was ready to take his father's place. He'd become a great warrior soon, and then she'd be the warrior's mother.

I won't be that. I'm sure of this, more sure than anything else in my whole long whittled-away life.

The thief tilted her head in thought, and she held her breath. It was ridiculous. This girl couldn't want an aging princess running off with her in search of adventure…

The thief drew her knife and crouched before the widow. "Fine. I'll try you out, partner." The knife moved, and her bonds fell away.

She smiled, and that smile grew to a grin, and that grin shone so bright it chased away the last shreds of fog. Nightwind whickered at her, and she went to his stall. "What do you think? Will you go on an adventure with me, old friend?"

He snuffled her hand in agreement, and accepted a treat.

It took only minutes to saddle him and a second horse for the thief. They led their mounts outside, and the night air smelled of far-away places: forests carpeted with ancient loam, the fresh bite of snow-draped peaks, and the distant, metallic tang of magic.

"Ready?" ask the thief.

"Let's go," she said.

They picked a direction, and rode.

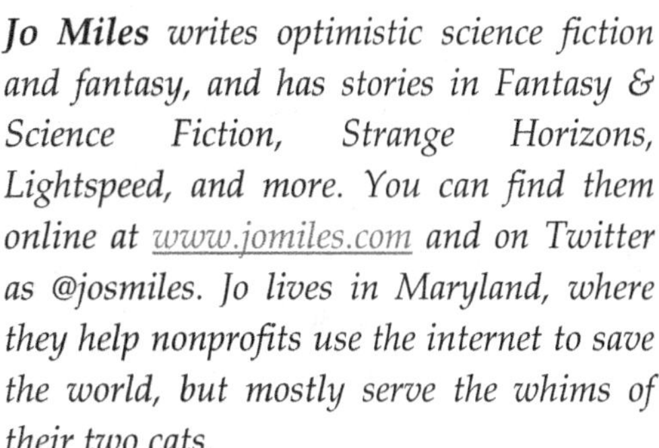

Jo Miles writes optimistic science fiction and fantasy, and has stories in Fantasy & Science Fiction, Strange Horizons, Lightspeed, and more. You can find them online at www.jomiles.com and on Twitter as @josmiles. Jo lives in Maryland, where they help nonprofits use the internet to save the world, but mostly serve the whims of their two cats.

The Golden Idol of the Dreadful Palace in the Hollywood Hills

Chloe Smith

It was three days since Chaz's last text, and the spectral fears of my anxiety ran feral and almost beyond my control. The longer his radio silence stretched, the more my stomach knotted. It wasn't ominous, I tried to tell myself. We weren't even officially dating. We were just friends who had taken acting classes together, who sometimes hooked up when he was between girlfriends. His silence didn't mean anything dire.

But by that third morning, the unending string of demands on the order board was the only thing that kept anxiety from strangling me. On the clock, with my hands busy and the hiss and squeal of the espresso machine filling my ears, I couldn't check my phone. I could tell myself that next time I looked, after my shift was over, surely there'd be an answering text at last. Maybe there'd be a call, even. Chaz's voice, warm and assured, telling me he was sorry he hadn't called; sorry I'd been worried....

I allowed myself to imagine I'd soon be back inside the magic circle of his golden-boy optimism, the cheerful aura that helped keep my many fears at bay. As long as I didn't look at my phone, I had the flimsy comfort of rationality: a belated reply message was much more likely than any of the other possibilities that hardened the air in my chest—that he'd been killed on one of the rollercoaster freeways, or stabbed in a liquor store, or run over while crossing the street.

I was good at this mind game, so good I felt almost calm as I doled out an unending string of cappuccinos and oat lattes with raw sugar. I rode that comfort until I stepped from behind the counter at the end of the morning rush. I shoved my rolled apron into my bag and dug out my phone, assurance plastered over my trepidation.

The price of cheating on fear, though, was that it rushed back, strengthened by the failure of my denials, when I finally stared down at reality of the empty screen.

My stomach roiled and the world faded amid a flurry of half-formed thoughts. *This can't be real.... If anything happened, I would have heard.... Maybe I should try again....* No. Calling and getting no answer would make it even worse. I squeezed my phone in one fist and closed my eyes against vertigo.

"He caught the eye of the Queen of Death, and dwells imprisoned in her dreadful palace."

The words were quiet but clear, despite the buzz of café noises. I opened my eyes to a shadow in front of me.

Not a shadow. A woman whose tall silhouette cut me off from the wider world, from the light shining in through the wide front windows. She had a curtain of dark hair and pale skin that might never have seen the LA sun before. She tilted her chin down at me, adjusted the wide rim of her sunglasses with one long fingered hand, waiting for me to speak.

"I'm sorry—what?"

"Your lover. He rests now in glory at the heart of her palace. He answered the call."

The café's clientele included its share of millenarians and fringe visionaries, but they were usually more beardy and stained, not coolly composed and clad in exquisite tailoring. The first part of what she said slid past me in a wave of cognitive dissonance. I focused on the last sentence, which almost made sense.

"An audition call? Are you—are you talking about Chaz? Chaz Billings?"

The slightest tip of her head. "Yes. He caught her notice and held it."

The spectral fears hesitated, retreated enough to let in hurt—Chaz was fine; he'd just landed some new offer, maybe the big one, the one that would lift him up and out of the life we shared: a life of obscurity and half-gnawed dreams, of years spent as an actor-slash-waiter, -slash-bartender, -slash-driver, -slash-anything-to-pay-the-bills while you scuttled along, chasing the high of possibility and ignoring the odds and the disappointments. He'd finally been pulled into that dazzling stratosphere, and hadn't even bothered to let me know....

I pushed away the bitterness, consciously chose skepticism: "If that's true, how would you know? And why tell me?"

The woman opened a clamshell pocketbook like something a Hepburn would carry and offered me a card. It was heavy, creamy stock, with edges so sharp they pricked at the tips of my fingers. *Lady Azrael* it read in curling font, and then, beneath that, *Talent*.

Then she said the magic words. The ones I'd been waiting years to hear.

"I think you have what I'm looking for."

After that, I was ready to accept anything. My fears had transformed, Furies to Eumenides, and now they made my heart stutter with hope and anticipation. She took me by the elbow, her touch cold against my skin.

"The Queen of Death requested diversion—some spark to enliven the eternal shadows of her court. She chose me, among all her angels, to seek out the next Inanna, the next Proserpina, the spirit or avatar who would quicken her cold halls. On her behalf, I journeyed through the infinite realms of mortal beliefs. I offered her dark-eyed sphinxes and ifrit princes, genius loci and superhuman folk heroes, but none would do. I despaired of pleasing her (and the despair of death is deep beyond all knowledge), and my failure gave hope to my rival—that upstart psychopomp, who covets my seat at the right hand of the Queen for his own."

I was listening for more phrases I recognized—projects, famous names, studios—but her words drew me farther and farther away from the familiar. They were a river whose current sucked me underground. "I don't—" I tried, but she kept going.

"Unbeknownst to me, he presented his own array of choices to our queen—and won her over. But only through the foulest disregard for the laws governing our realm." For a moment, shadowy wings spread behind her. I would have jerked away, if it wasn't for the iron vise of her grip. "He brought mortals—living mortals before our queen. Of course, among the hosts of the dead, life would shine brightly enough to warm any watcher. But it is *wrong*."

She paused, drew a breath, focused on me again. "I am sorry, mortal. This should not be your concern, but boundaries between the living and the dead, the flesh and spirit, those are the pillars that support our worlds. My Queen has been betrayed. Offered living entertainment, she is now besotted with the vision of life that breathes before her. She will not see reason."

I couldn't look away from her, though the anxious, restless part of me wondered if anyone else had noticed an Angel of Death in the corner of a crowded café. But self-consciousness didn't stop me from asking, "What does Chaz have to do with all this?"

She smiled, with infinity behind her eyes. "My rival, in all his misguided cleverness, put out a call for a young Adonis, and selected your Chaz from the teeming pack. Now he dwells at the heart of my Queen's fortress, and woe betide us all."

This was insane—or else some elaborate performance art or staged method acting experiment. And yet, her words and her presence pulled at me, asserting their own reality. If there was any possibility that Chaz was truly trapped, a prisoner in some uncanny "fortress" …. I realized I was knotting my hands together, as if in supplication. "How can I get him back?"

"I'm so glad you asked." The words rang in the space between us, but I didn't have time to ponder the menace beneath their satisfaction. She went on, "I have no power to retrieve the living from the realm of the dead; my gifts lie entirely in the world beyond. Only another mortal can call him back, one who knows and cares for him. Is that you?"

I nodded, breathless. "Yes—I'll do it."

"Good." She stepped past me and I followed, almost skipping to keep up with her strides. Outside, she stopped at a low, sleek car, idling at the curb.

"I can lead you across the veil and into the court tonight. The address is on the back of the card. Be there at sundown."

She slid into the passenger seat and disappeared behind a pane of tinted glass, leaving me staring into the rush of traffic under a sun that was suddenly scorching.

I didn't recognize the address, but my navigation app swallowed it without comment. My phone's robotic voice directed me to roads that traced the canyon ridges north of Hollywood. My car revved and complained at the grades, and I leaned over the wheel, looking for numbers or street signs in the rising dusk, until I spotted the box shape of a gatehouse. Its windows glowed already, although skyline above the trees was still salmon-bright.

I parked beyond the drive, ashamed of my scuffed economy sedan, and walked into the circle of the gatehouse's light. I was surprised how little fear I felt: the voices of my spectral anxieties were muted by the unreality of it all.

The man within the gatehouse was old, so wasted that his guard's uniform crumpled over his bony form. One spindly hand gripped the edge of the doorframe, as if he could barely stay upright, even seated in his chair. His skin sagged beneath his eyes and in folds at his neck

"Excuse me, I'm here to—well, Lady Azrael invited me…." I fumbled in my purse.

He frowned up at me. "You have the fare?"

"Well, not exactly." I held out her card.

He sighed and looked away. "They forget the traditions, these children of a lesser age. Forget what is owed…." His words vanished into another sigh, and he began to climb to his feet, limbs trembling.

"Oh, no, sir; you don't have to—" I reached forward in concern, but then froze as he began to unfold.

He straightened limbs long and spidery enough that my head tilted back to take him in. His skin tightened around his skull bones, eyes deepening into their hollows. He reached out towards where I had frozen in place. "You have no coin to pay the ferry man…."

"That is enough of that!"

The Lady Azrael was suddenly there, interposed between the two of us. Her precision-cut suit had been replaced with a fall of white silk that sheathed her body but left her shoulders bare. Her heavy hair swung forward and then back as she nodded, and then the gate guard was a bent old man again, looking as us through watery eyes. She told him, "This is not a mere soul crossing over; she is my guest."

He harrumphed and slumped down in his seat, frowned out into the empty, shadowed street. Lady Azrael took my arm to guide me, and her touch this time was like the cold of the ocean. It bit into my bones. She drew me forward, down into the bowl of a manicured garden. I glimpsed the shape of the house beyond it, but within a few steps we were moving through a maze of gravel paths and artfully shaped hedges. They stretched away from us in all directions, fading into grey nothingness. I tried to look back towards the gatehouse and the vanished street, but the Lady jerked at my arm.

"Listen." For the first time, her words sounded urgent. "I can bring you through the outer veils, but when it comes to recalling your lover, my hands are tied. You must reach him and convince him to return on your own."

"Convince him?" I tried to ask, but her voice ran over mine.

"Most important, if we are separated and you have to go on alone, without the benefit of my protection, know this: you walk through the halls of Death, which no mortal can withstand for long. A score of heartbeats, perhaps a few more, and then your life will be forfeit, unless you have returned to the outer world before then."

I tried to balk. "There's nothing I can do in twenty heartbeats. That's not even a minute!"

"Foolish child," she ducked to pass under the curve of a topiary arch, "Time does not have the same meaning here—"

Her words cut off as she emerged on the other side, and the grip I'd been resisting fell away. Another figure stood before her, blocking the path that now stretched across a swath of grass like black velvet. He was as tall as Lady Azrael, and beautiful as well, but lovely the way a horned beetle is, or a Portuguese man o'war: compelling and horrifying. White moth wings fluttered from the back of a form that was angular as a runway model's. His wide-set eyes narrowed. "And you scorned me for bringing living mortals, sister?"

"Apollyon." Azrael drew herself up. "If anything, your tricks have driven me to desperate measures."

His mouth twisted. "So much for your fine words—scorning to commingle the living and the dead. 'The threat to the natural order'"—even in his alien voice, I could hear the sardonic quotation marks—"Did you compel her with principled argument? Pretend that your dissatisfaction was about more that royal favor?" His gaze slid past her and found mine. "What honey sop did she use to tempt you here?"

My fears came uncoiled within me, and the look I threw at Azrael must have telegraphed some of their urgency. "I didn't lie to you, child," she said, "Your lover is here, and you can save him."

"No!" Apollyon threw up a hand in warning. "He is my tribute to our queen, here under my protection. Just because you could not divert her with your chimeras, does not mean that you can manufacture Orpheus out of some malleable clay."

Azrael hissed, a low, inhuman sound that touched some prey instinct in my brainstem and made me cower away from her as well. "Graveling! You have never earned the right hand of our queen."

Apollyon's smirk was the most human thing about him. "And yet I have pleased her with my offering. If only you had thought of a better diversion sooner—"

Lady Azrael crouched and, with stomach-turning suddenness, her white dress flared and uncoiled, becoming wings that mantled over her shoulders, not moth-ragged but pinioned and sharp. Her form changed as well, muscles cording and fingers curling into claws. One of those clawed hands reached out and shoved me away. *"Remember! A score of heartbeats."*

The words echoed in my head, persisted over her shriek as she launched herself at Apollyon. He leaped to meet her, and I winced away from the sound of their contact, even as I fled across the lawn.

The expanse of grass was like sand or mud: it dragged at my feet as I tried to hurry. I glanced over my shoulder once, but the struggle between the two Angels of Death was nothing more than a flurry of movements in the dark behind me. I looked forward again, and saw the walls of the house rising before me, somehow no closer than it had been when I started running. I put my head down and staggered on, my breath rasping in my throat. There was no way I would reach the house in twenty heartbeats, or two hundred. I should just lie down and accept death now.

Instead, I kicked off my heels and pushed myself harder. The ground was dry beneath my bare soles, but it still sucked at them. One more step. Another. The effort was like pushing through honey.

Then my toe stubbed against the sharp edge of a brick patio, and the drag on my body loosened. I flailed forwards for a few paces before catching myself. For a moment I stood, lungs heaving, expecting to feel my heart burst within my chest—but it was still. I waited, and my breath quieted in the listening, immediately slow and even, as if I hadn't just been running for my life. *Is this death?* I wondered.

Then I felt it. One slow, low heartbeat. Then nothing. Instinct made me want to wait for another, to prove I was still alive—but that was lost time I couldn't get back. I fisted my hands at my sides, looked up at what was ahead.

The house's wings stretched in both directions, with tall windows full of light that should have fallen outwards, illuminating the night. Instead, their glow was cold, anemic, the view within blocked by curtains like Apollyon's fluttering wings.

Directly ahead of me, a floor-to ceiling window stood half open. I crossed the stretch of patio and slipped inside, between the folds of drapery, into the Fortress of Death.

Inside, everything is white and black: walls, furniture, clothing. People with skin like newsprint and cigarette ash, dressed in slick midnight silks and ermine furs. Everyone is so still and quiet that my next heartbeat sounds like a gong in my ears and makes me jump. I freeze again, sure that the crowd who fill the room will turn at the disturbance— but no one seems to notice. It is a long, high-ceilinged space, and they are scattered across it: seated on low-slung couches or leaning artfully against the full bar, gathered in knots and pairs like any partygoers at such a mansion, except for their stillness, their faded expressions. I hesitate, catch myself doing so, and then go forward again, down the few steps to the tiled floor.

I walk between the shades whose stillness seems to shift and then settle back in the wake of my passing. I go from room to room—grand entry hall, ballroom, bedrooms—looking for Chaz, even for another Angel, for Death herself, for something beyond these insubstantial, unresponsive forms. My heartbeats pass, slowly.

I count twelve before I find him.

It's another white-paneled, black pillared room. This one has a sunken floor framed by broad steps, like an amphitheater. There is even a stage-like platform at the center, and around its circumference sit more shades, their eyes turned up in wonder. Among them, in a central, high-backed chair directly opposite me, sits a woman with perfectly symmetrical beauty: dark skin, eyes like the depths of the sea, a crown of gilded braids. She is as still as stone, as still as silence, but her cheeks are curved with a gentle, terrifying half-smile as she looks at me.

Between us, on the platform, is Chaz.

He is the only thing here not still, faded, or pale. He is underdressed for the setting, in the clothes I last saw him wearing—worn jeans and a tight graphic tee that shows off the body he's worked hard to maintain. I know his agent (who's also mine, when I can get ahold of her) tries to pitch him as a "younger, lither Channing Tatum"—which even I thought was a bit of a stretch. But now he makes the idea of star status literal rather than aspirational. He glows. The power of his vitality, of his *aliveness* is a golden light that radiates off of his skin. He is like amber, like a glass of apple wine held up to the sun. I can feel the way his life warms the shades clustered around him. It draws me, too. I take a half step forward.

The sound makes him turn, and his face lights up even more when he sees me. He leaps from the stage and up the steps towards me, as shades flutter and fall back from his path.

"Lucy!" He embraces me, and the warmth, the reality of him, is almost overpowering. He releases me, but keeps hold of my hands.

"Chaz," I look up into his face. "I've come to rescue you."

I don't know what response I expected, but it isn't this. He frowns, puzzled, and the light of him dims ever so slightly. "Huh?"

"To rescue you—bring you back," I glance down towards the crowned figure, feeling suddenly exposed. She hasn't moved or changed her serene expression. Still, I lower my voice, "to, you know, home. The, the *land of the living*."

Somehow, the phrase sounds foolish, campy, even in the midst of this undeniably mythic place. Chaz's lips quirk, but he nods, slowly, as if struggling to remember. "...Right, the place beyond this place. The industry. The dream."

"Yes!" I tug on his hands, take a step backwards and towards the exit.

He resists my pull. "Why?"

Now it's my turn to be puzzled. "What do you mean 'why'? To be free. To be alive!" I yank him again.

"But I am alive," His face breaks into a smile again. "I'm the most alive person here." He shoots a glance around at the silent, faded audience.

I understand, suddenly. I know because I've hungered to be chosen, to be recognized, myself. But not like this— never like this.

"And you'd live imprisoned and surrounded by the dead." I mean to snarl, to shock him into response, but my words come out softer, regretful. In this place outside of time, my realization has already happened, will happen, is happening now. The decision I can see firming behind his eyes was made before we ever spoke. The inevitability of his golden brilliance was always the most important thing in his life.

I feel the thud of my heart, reminding me that I'm not yet beyond time's pull—although its grip is slipping. I've lost count of the beats. Chaz frowns and reaches out an amber finger to brush the corner of my jaw, just above the hollow where my pulse rang. Maybe he sensed it too, in this house of stillness.

"You could stay," he says.

I think of Lady Azrael's promise. "I didn't get the contract offer you did. I would be just another shade."

He actually shrugs. "There's no fear here."

He's right. For everyone here, the worst thing possible has already happened. That comfort, the absence of "what if?" tempts me, and he knows it. He's always understood my weaknesses. And understood how I needed him.

I can see that now.

I step back, up another of the risers. Chaz lets me go. His eyes slide away from me, towards the crowd that still watch him, rapt. I look past him, towards the dark Queen. Her gaze alone is fixed on me, fell and terrifying.

She sees me poised on the knife-edge of fear and want.

She nods once, meditatively. Unsurprised. Death is patient, inevitable.

Before I realize I've made my decision, I've turned away. I feel Death's eyes on me, but I don't know if Chaz notices me go.

I don't feel my heart beat again until my fingers are pushing through and past the heavy curtains, until I am—

—until I *was* running, flying across the stretch of lawn and away. As I cut through the shadowed garden, my breath tightened and my heart labored at last. Shadows moved in the air above me, and I ducked my head, afraid to see if Azrael and Apollyon still fought, or if the victor was swooping down to try and arrest my flight.

Once past the now-dark shape of the gatehouse, though, I forced my uneven, barefoot steps to slow. I could feel my spectral fears hovering, tightening the corners of my mind. They were never far away—inescapable as the face of Death. They were part of me.

I let them hover, and kept walking, careful in the dark, all the way back to my car.

Chloe Smith teaches English and history to 14-year-olds, which is never boring. Besides teaching, she works as a proofreader for Fantasy magazine, and writes science fiction and fantasy stories whenever she can make the time. She was born and raised in the San Francisco Bay Area, and she lived in Texas and Washington states, New York City, and rural France before coming back to California. Her short fiction has appeared in Metaphorosis, Three-Lobed Burning Eye, Interzone Digital, and elsewhere. Her debut novella, Virgin Land, is out from Luna Press Publishing in February 2023

Noctes ambrosianae by Walter Sickert

Noctes

Billy Stanton

Globules of paint; smeared oils, circular strokes standing in for faces, pale pigments infused with flecks and valleys and shadows of sow-hide pink, gold like a dirty trumpet, ancient cave-wall brown, clementine orange and Dury Lane puddle-grey. Black eyes glower; they are diamonds from the crown of the reclining Britannia of resurgent dirty Empire, coal lumps for the ships and trains run on hellfire. A sinister singular intelligence is spread across this mass of people turned simian; writhing and rolling and undulating like a snake or a heckling Hydra, silent screaming and lost gibbon jeering, suggesting hyena viciousness going unheard. Other painters of the time loved the crowd, were moved by it, excited by it, and saw the future in it. Instead, this is worse than Poe. This is the end; the curse; a streaking of the irredeemable land after the fall, blighted and blasted, always cold and hungry.

The black balcony has a gold finish: it is like a coffin for Sickert's sickness, a depository for the shadow-plays and human-puppet shows of London. We glimpse common desires twisted and made lupine under the weight of suppression, the dark sun around the back of the golden orb, the black half of the supernatural moon, and the empty misery of space. Somewhere unseen is the actor or the singer on the stage, withering beneath her red petticoats, trying to hold back her angry trembling while flanked by a chorus-line of flesh being destroyed by the eyes of these men and boys (only men and boys), night after night. Surely there would be an unexpected quaver in the voice that delivered the final punchline of the cheap comic song, a frosted-glass crack in the light operetta junk facade; how could there not be?

At the centre of the scene of onlookers is the face: the face I know, the face I hate. It is more alien than the rest; it is larger and more deformed, little more than a pulsating mangling of raw meat sculpted into the approximate shape of a human head. It gazes out with white eyes, hard and angry and merciless, and tries to disguise itself beneath a black cap and a blue scarf. There was awfulness all up and down the stalls that night, hanging from every rung of the balcony, but in that face, it is concentrated; it is given true corporeal form; it is an oasis of still and brooding hate in this manically loathing zoo of England. It is no accident, no forgery, no act of imagination on the part of dear Walter; the face was there that night in the music hall and so Sickert put it where it had been. He didn't know quite the extent of what he was doing; this is the man of many rumours, Cornwell's Ripper, but all that is conjecture born of the unique violence of his paintings. Sickert secretly sought out the truly horrible through a network of studio-dens in the filthy corners of the city, and in public houses where the rear alleyways formed open-air brothels for gentlemen and dockers alike, but only once did he actually encounter it. Only once did he manage to put the real pure thing on canvas, as it was and as it is.

With every fibre of my being, I loath this painting and have done ever since I first saw it at the age of fourteen in a provincial art gallery. For thirty-eight years, however, I have had the same print of it pinned to a wall in every single bedsit, flat and hotel room I have inhabited. By now, it is speckled with mould and dirt, as well as creased and bent and covered in the corners with tiny holes where it has been pierced many times with thumbtacks. It is, in many ways, the prize of my life; my lonely life conducted with red-rimmed eyes; my life almost as threatened and haunted and humiliated as this masterpiece. An Intelligence Officer with intelligence he can't share; intelligence he must never share. It is a bitter irony, but a common one, in different variations than my own.

My true secret, my biggest and most laughable secret, distinct from the petty chess moves of powerful men's egos, is that twice I have seen the evil come out that painting and I await, every single day, every single night, the third occasion.

It seems to happen when the temperature drops below zero; when cars crunch through gravelly sleet sludge; when the gritters fail on their midnight rounds.

The first time, the snow was piled high in the gutters of the capitol's western avenues and the pavement was marked out in one central line of treacherous thin black ice. I was working with a colleague in a house near the National Gallery in Trafalgar Square. A small apartment had been leased to a double agent, and we were installing a number of recording devices in the sash-window frames in time for his meeting with his controller in two days. The room was like a morgue. It had long been unoccupied, and as much as sash windows are coveted as authentic treasures of tradition, they are draughty bastards. The wind picked at our busy fingers even through our leather gloves; every breath produced a thick cloud of condensation, adding to a collection that seemed to dominate the room, hiding the corners behind a shimmering haze. Collinson told me to go for a walk to warm up. It was against protocol, but we were on the verge of freezing to death.

I went to the National, even though it was evening and only forty-five minutes or so before late Christmas closing. Trafalgar Square was busy with the gift-buying throngs. I ruined a dozen tourist photographs as I stalked through the backgrounds of their shots like a spectre of old respectable England, clutching my leather suitcase and cocooned in my long black coat. Inside the building, almost every gallery was deserted. I flashed my membership card at the entrance to an exhibition of British paintings inspired by the Impressionists. Within, the walls were painted in dull crimson and navy and the dim electric lights hardly made the gold frames of the best-regarded canvases glisten. The corridors were long and mournful and echoing; paintings exploded with movement and colour, the gaiety and tragedy of life filtered through eyes tainted by the perceptions of bourgeois Parisians, but it was all gone from this place. I felt like I was back in the frozen room, breathing smoke like a dragon and listening to the murmurings of light entertainment television playing in the downstairs flat.

The Sickert's were displayed in the middle of the exhibition. There was his scene from Hove seafront, two pensioners talking on a bench beside a glowering white seaside hotel palace; there were the gloomy shopfronts of London and Dieppe, busy with bric-a-brac; there were the fauvist Brighton Pierrots, coloured violently for the dawn of trench warfare; there were those snapshots of Minnie Cunningham mid-performance, presented as if Degas had been gorging on gothic novels. And there was '*Noctes ambrosianae* '(1906, oil on canvas), on loan from its home gallery. I stood before it, stunned to see it again, richer, sicklier and more yellow than in any reproduction. I looked at it for a long time, avoiding that face I knew was in the centre; that face which I stared at through the night, trying to puzzle it out as it peered from my bedroom wall. I couldn't bear the face in person; the feeling coming from it was too strong. It filled the room like my stagnant breath in the safe-house.

I finally tore myself away and turned my back. I didn't see it until I was ready to leave the room; when I took one final look back at those paintings which I was likely not to enjoy again until the next Sickert exhibition came around in a decade or two. Then I saw that the face, indeed the entire creature, had come out from the picture. Where it had stood in the crowd was only a blank space, a smear of brownish paint. In the room, in the flesh, it stood in its cap and scarf, with its white eyes blank and dull, and the skin of its face a puckered and pockmarked swirl of pink-and-red, like that of an atom bomb victim. It was as silent as it had been in oil but not as motionless. It swung and waved its arms around manically and seemed to be dancing a jig with its legs bending and twisting. The only sound came from the squeak of leather shoes across the varnished wooden floor.

I ran from the room. I ran through the gallery. I sprinted past the cleaners beginning their shifts in the lobby and back to the safe-house, spoiling more tourist photographs and knocking pedestrians bandy. I cared not for secrecy; I gave no thought as to who may be seeing me re-enter the flat. It did not matter anyway; Collinson was dead. He'd been garrotted with a piano wire still lying on the frayed ochre carpet beside his corpse. The windows had been smashed and the sash frames obliterated. The assassins either hadn't known Collinson wasn't alone or not bothered to wait for his partner; he was far more senior than me, anyway, and had turned some big names, claimed some real scalps. Collinson was more dangerous; Collinson knew more; Collinson was neutralised.

The second time I saw it was about eight years later. I had bought suspicion on myself by leaving my partner to his fate, despite doing so at his insistence, and I was continuing my career in relative anonymity, the closest thing the service has to a complete pencil-pusher. There would be no more for-your-eyes-only's, no more mastering, no more games.

Sunk into a deep depression, I occupied a second-floor room in a five-storey building that must have been one of London's last true boarding houses: the kind that was not a hotel or somewhere with a tenancy agreement. It was the sort of place where loners and losers came to stay for uncertain periods of months or years, and I was now a loner and a loser. I drank and smoked in my bedsit far from the old members clubs and even the cheap bars. Each night, as I sat up in my insomniac's dry-hypnagogia, I stared at the pink swirl in the old print. I willed it to step out from the glossy paper. I wanted it to come and explain what had happened that night, to confirm that what I had experienced in the National was not the feverish hallucinations of a man unknowingly stricken from exposure and collapsing in on himself from being trapped in that icebox of a living room but a true visitation.

It took a very long time, but it came one January. There was no snow; only a blistering rain, sharp and heavy as it rattled against the windows and capable of cutting chunks from the bare flesh of any late-night lout traipsing back from the pub. I sat in my old monogrammed pyjamas gifted by my mother, an anachronism again. As I watched, the reproduction slowly curled in one corner, then another, becoming a cylinder that popped free of its final thumbtacks and fell to the floor. I crawled to the end of the bed to pick the piece up; its snail-pace movements had held me mesmerised, but I felt no fear or expectation of anything unusual. But as I looked over the bed's foot, the print unfurled itself and lay image-side up. In the picture, the creature stirred; in subtly jerking movements, like those of rudimentary stop-motion animation, it propelled itself forwards utilising the heads of the two men beside itself as leverage. Soon, the torso of the thing filled the entire canvas, and then it was in my room, standing atop the picture and staring at me in my bed. Neither of us moved for a long while; I cowered under the spell of its look. Its hate penetrated me at every angle; it burned in my lungs, it threatened to tear my ribcage apart, and it ran up and down my spine like an electric shock. I eventually started to twitch and then to convulse, thrashing about on the bedclothes and sweating so much that the scent of my own rancid musk was all I could smell. As if to mock me, the beast began again the performance of the gallery. It swung its arms and jigged around. Its mouth- or what counted as its mouth- hung open in a silent scream or laugh that showed as a deep, dark and perfect hole in the lower-third of its head. Little stars seemed to glimmer in the hole, constellations of unknown names and size.

Then the creature bent down, picked the print from the floor, tacked it again to the wall, and clambered back inside, using the wooden beams of my bed frame as a boost. I fainted dead away, as they say, and dreamed hard. I floated in my striped pyjamas through the constellations in the thing's mouth, the universes behind its ruined flesh. I was cold and warm and joyful and frightful. I knew nothing and everything and savoured it. I learnt something of this being's nature, its motivations, but not enough- never enough.

When I awoke, I was being led from my bed and held on one side by a policeman and on the other by a paramedic. They took me to the pavement outside, where the rest of the house's residents were clustered around a couple of ambulances, watched on by most of the rest of the locals in this corner of Bloomsbury. The roof had caved in on the two linked top-floor bedrooms. The four boys staying in these rooms had all been day-labourers employed constructing some university building across Russell Square; two lads from Rotherham and Rochdale, a German and a Pole. They were all dead.

So I hate the painting and I treasure it. I do not know fully what manner of thing it is that crawls from it, but I know it brings death with it and that it wants me to understand this. Does this creature save or torment its greatest admirer, this man who would burn the painting if he could but infiltrate the gallery and tear it from the wall? I cannot tell. But it is part of me or all of me, the entirety, the whole, the bastard of myself. It is the hate of the crowd; the hate of the individual; the hate of Sickert; the hate of an era; the hate of all eras; the hate of

England. It is the vengeful cackle behind the gag that plays to the stalls; it is the knife that was in the abdomen of the prostitutes; it is the blood that was soon to be spread on the poppy-fields, when the cannons blasted so that Walter could hear them across the channel on a clear night; it is the piano wire around Collinson's throat and the debris that crushed the men as they slept; it is the roaring when a man is reduced to an animal and forced to live in and as dirt; it is the paintbrush that erases what was there as it immortalises it. It has been fifteen years, but I will see that swirl of a face in the flesh again. It is inevitable.

The painting is a summation, the final word, the full stop at the end of a sentence, and is a door left open.

Billy Stanton *is a young working-class writer and filmmaker based in London, and originally from Portsmouth. His story 'Screwfix' was recently published in the 'New Towns' anthology (Wild Pressed Books). His short fiction has also appeared in Horla, The Chamber and Tigershark magazines. His latest short film 'Noli' is currently in post-production. His blog can be found at: steelcathedrals.wordpress.com*

The Bearable Fragility of Ordinary Things
Elisabeth Ring

It had been about two weeks now and Ento was starting to get the hang of the whole being-made-from-glass thing. It helped that the autumn was mild, so far, so he didn't have to worry about temperature fluctuations. So did the whole string of rules he'd made for himself.

Rule one: Only walk on grass or moss or very thick blankets of leaves wherever possible.

Rule two: If forced to walk on dirt, avoid pebbles. If forced to walk on cobblestone, tread very, very carefully.

The day it all happened, when he and the rest of the village took stock of what that burst of chaos magic did to them, Ina the blacksmith's daughter pointed at him and gasped.

"Look at him!" she said, her new tentacle hair writhing with amazement. "He's made of diamond!"

He *did* look precious, hard and clear and gleaming in the sunlight. He watched as bright spots the light passing through him made on the ground, and the other villagers marveled at him. When those spots of light made some of the drier leaves at his feet combust, the closer villagers did take a step back, but they remained in awe of him. (That was another rule: Don't go out at midday if it can be helped.) Ina in particular paid more attention to him those three hours than he remembered her giving him in total the entire nineteen years before. Who knew what might have happened if he hadn't stubbed his foot on a loose cobblestone in the market road.

Ento was well-acquainted with stubbing toes, bashing his shins, and otherwise colliding with his environment in new and painful ways. This time, there was no pain, only the sudden stop of his foot and the lurch as his momentum carried him where that foot was supposed to have gone. But there was a high *clink* that didn't register to his ears until he stumbled himself back to uprightness. The lack of a throbbing toe seemed good fortune, one that couldn't be claimed by the candlemaker's wife, whose every uttered word now made feathers pour from her lips and drift lazily to the ground before her. Yet when he glanced down, Ento noticed a divot in the glass toe of his boot and a faint crack running up from it. He was not diamond, then, but glass.

Ina kept quite a distance from him after that. Which really wasn't fair, because glass was valuable, too, if not as sturdy. And it wasn't as if others didn't have it worse—what about the merchant's son, whose sweat now smelled like sulfur? Or the elderly apothecary's wife, whose feet had turned to horse's hooves? Ento had found it hard to feel emotion since turning into glass, but it was hard not to worry. He was no paragon of gracefulness, nor did he have the luxury of staying inside where comparatively little could hurt him, like some mayor's child or minor noble. He was the sort who was supposed to work until he died, just as his father had, though the work wasn't what killed him. Made of diamond, Ento could have ploughed fields or hauled fishing nets or even gone into the mines without fear. But glass? What could he do made of glass?

At present, he was running errands for those too embarrassed about their new conditions to go into the market. On one arm, Ento carried an empty basket from the spinner to be filled with eggs even more fragile than he was. Tucked under the other was a bag of feathers collected by the candlemaker's wife to be sold at market as stuffing for pillows and mattresses.

"They had an argument last night," whispered the candlemaker's neighbor, the orchard keeper, as Ento paused at his house. The neighbor, whose orchards hung heavy with unpicked fruit, had stuck a brown-furred hand out the door with a little satchel of coins. "Some bread and cheese, please, and as many shaving razors as you can get."

That satchel was now stuffed in Ento's pants pocket, and clinked softly along with each careful step. It seemed strange to Ento to be wearing his ratty old pants and shirt over the much-nicer pants and shirt and boots he'd been wearing that day the band of fighters traipsed through town on their way to the wizard's tower. But what he'd been wearing that day was turned to glass with him. Sometimes at night, he would run a glass finger across the smooth shape between wrist and cuff, or on the zig-zag of his boots' laces he would have tied much neater that day had he known he'd be wearing them forever just like so. Wearing the second set of clothes kept him from risking setting fire to every dry leaf, and the fact people could no longer see through him made him feel like more of a person. Also, they gave him pockets. He was saving up, penny by penny, for a pair of large new boots he could wear over his boot-shaped feet. Maybe then he could walk faster and fear the cobblestones less.

One good thing, at least for Ento, that had come about since that day was a dramatic drop in the number of horses and goats and other animals roaming the market. Part of this had to do with how many people were adjusting privately to their new selves, or had less need for daily goods—Ento, for one, hadn't felt hunger yet, so he had that going for him, though his grandmother still needed to eat. But livestock hadn't been immune from the burst of magic, either. Some things were harmless or even beneficial, such as the miller's horse sprouting an udder like a cow's. Other changes were more detrimental to carrying on as usual, such as the wheat farmer's team, one of which had shrunk to the size of a cat and the other had sprouted gills and thrown itself into the pond. Ento had heard at least one of the cheesemaker's cows now gave wine, so it seemed a change of occupation was likely in order. The overall state of the market, though, meant Ento had a far lower chance of being kicked by some ornery goat or knocked aside by someone galloping a horse recklessly through the square. Before, he would have been banged up well enough, but now he would surely shatter.

"It's not forever, though," said Loy, a farmhand Ento had worked with a few times before, and Ento's ears pricked at the outskirts of the conversation as he slowly passed the young men gathered near a small collection of barrels. Back then, Loy had been most notable for his quick hands that could free the plow from even the thickets tangles of weeds in seconds. Now, his most notable feature were his ears, hanging down to his neck as dark and silky as a rabbit's. "Just until someone sets it right."

Telden, who rowed the ferry across the river, scoffed and his thick, scaly tail twitched. "Who's going to set this right?"

"Well, think about it: We're this way because those fighters killed the old wizard," Loy said.

"Finally," muttered another farmhand, Dran, whose skin had been turned a lovely shade of dappled purple.

He had a point: for as long as Ento could remember—for as long as *anyone* could remember, except maybe Ento's gram, on one of her good days—the wizard had occupied the tall tower outside of the village, and bands of aspiring heroes had come through with the explicit intent to slay him. A few managed to get out now and then, and Ento would see them running away bleeding and terrified. Sometimes the groups would bring in large weapons drawn in a wagon—or that one band, when Ento was twelve, that dragged an ogre behind them by a rope around its neck. A very *weak* rope; the ogre pulled back and snapped the rope in two, and its resulting rampage killed seven villagers. Among them, Ento's father, Toren. Luck had never run in the family.

"The way I heard it," Loy continued, "that wizard got his power from some kind of well of magic, and when they killed him, whatever control he had over it was lost, resulting in..." He gestured to his ears, Dran's skin, Telden's tail. "So if there's all that magic for the taking, somebody's going to want to come around and take it, right? And if we're this way because of lost magic, they're going to want it back."

Telden's tail thumped softly against the barrel. "Yeah, but magic's not like sheep—you can't just gather it up when it gets out. It's more like water, see? You splash it on the ground and the dirt soaks it up."

"You're saying we're the dirt?" Dran asked.

Telden shrugged. "All I know is I'm not counting on anything changing back."

"What if we went up there?" Dran asked. "Saw for ourselves, at least, if there was any way to un-soak this magic, or whatever happened. See if we can go back to normal."

Normal. Normal had been boring. Normal had seen Ento as a trifle, practically invisible. Now, normal seemed like a distant dream. But Dran didn't have it so bad being normal. Neither did the other two, judging by how quickly their discussion turned to planning how to climb what remained of the tower. Ento paused, a distant thrill twirling up his chest. He could go with them. He could help make this go away—or he could, if he'd been transformed into sturdier stuff. Back when everything was normal, the other boys wouldn't let him in on the games of tackle ball they'd play when someone had a fresh pig's bladder to blow up. Too fragile, they'd said; he'd break the first time one of them looked at him. Now…

At least some things were still the same.

A flutter of wings and a too-close squawk interrupted Ento's slow-moving eavesdropping. He stopped and looked around wildly for the source. Rule four: Avoid projectiles at all costs. That included dive-bombing birds. He saw nothing but the farmer's wife slapping an old bedsheet on the ground, cheeks flushed with exertion. She pulled the sheet back up with a swirl of dust and slapped it back down again. This time, a chicken-sized lump kept the dirty sheet from lying flat on the ground.

"Erd-riech p'dom," she murmured. As near as anyone could tell, the magic had changed all her words to the Forgotten Tongue, which probably meant she could get into some sealed-up caves or castles or something. Not that there were any of those around here. She scooped up the invisible chicken, which strained against the dirty sheet, and said, "O'nej."

Ento didn't know any Forgotten Tongue, but it was easy enough to tell what she meant. "It's all right," he said.

He usually tried not to speak, with the crystalline ring his voice had to it now, but the farmer's wife seemed like a safe one to speak to. Besides no one understanding a word she said, her once-high, clear timbre now had a deep echo to it, like someone was shouting a spell across a chasm. If there was anyone who would understand what it was to not sound like yourself, it was her. But when she glanced around to make sure she didn't run into anyone, he avoided looking at her eyes. They had been changed, too, turned all black but for the constellations winking within them, and even he filled with panic at the sight of them.

The feathers were easy enough to sell to the merchant. With so many feathers now on hand without having to pluck them, Ento wondered how long it would be until the whole village slept on feather beds. He kept the coins he got for the feathers in their own pocket so they wouldn't get jumbled up with those meant to be used on the orchard keeper's goods.

"Razors? Again?" asked the merchant, scratching his beard with a clawed finger. Behind the stall, Ento thought he could see a twitch of Ina's tentacles. "I just sold him about all my stock last week. I got three left but won't get in any more until the end of the month."

Ento shifted, feet clinking disconcertingly on the cobblestones. "You won't sell him what you have?" he asked as low as he could. Whispering made the ringing sound worse.

The merchant considered, then let out a long sigh. "All right, but tell him to be more careful with these until the end of the month, or he'll have to start stealing from other people's homes."

With a nod, Ento carefully counted out the correct amount (Rule five: Be very careful when picking up anything metal or stone), then put the razors sharp-side up in his pocket, but more to protect the pocket than himself from an accidental cut. He could chip, he could shatter, but it would take a lot to cut him.

Despite one cow giving wine instead of milk, the cheesemaker had cheese enough to sell. A line at the baker's made him linger at the fringes, watching a small menagerie of spell-altered customers get their bread until he felt safe enough to exchange coin for a loaf himself. There were plenty of eggs to be had, and big ones, too, since one of the hens had grown to the size of a dog. The farmer's wife took the money from the basket's bottom and silently filled it with eggs, an orange cat coiling around her ankles.

Ento waited, watching and listening to the villagers who could still act as carefree as he had once been. Across the road, the apothecary's wife stood in the blacksmith's shop, hands resting on the shoulder-high stall. The blacksmith held the shoe in place with two hands, the nail with another, and brought the hammer down with a fourth.

The apothecary's wife flinched at the sound of hammer striking nail against her hoof. "It doesn't hurt," she said, "but it does feel so strange—like someone pushing against the white of your nail, only it's not..." She paused, flinched again. "But it doesn't hurt."

The blacksmith and his wife exchanged a series of glances, brows quirking and heads tilting in silent conversation. The blacksmith's gaze slid to Ento briefly, then darted back to his wife. Rumor was the same magic that had given him twice the hands and twice the legs had also doubled his tongue and he had not yet found a way to talk with it.

"He says he can do it more softly if you'd like," said the blacksmith's wife after a moment, "but it might take longer."

"He can carry on; I'll take strangeness over getting a pebble in my feet again," said the apothecary's wife, and gripped the low half-wall of the stable, bracing for the next blow.

A nudge at his arm made him turn— the farmer's wife, holding out a full basket of eggs. Beside her, the cat stretched, yawned, revealing a mouth filled with teeth: rows in the usual place, plus spines on its tongue and the roof of its mouth. It must be a good mouser now, if it wasn't before. Ento took the basket, nodding in thanks.

Arms laden with goods, Ento left the market, his steps feeling freer on the grass than they had on stone. Back to the orchard keeper's with too few razors and some of his money left unspent. Back to the candlemaker's wife and the profit brought by their argument. When he reached the spinner's house, he found a coin on the front stoop and assumed he was to leave the basket in its place. Through the door, he thought he could hear the snoring of beasts—the spinner had many children, and the magic had done different things to them all. And finally, back to his own little house with the coins he'd made from his deliveries.

"Toren? You're home early," said Ento's gram, hunched over her knitting by the fire. Her words warbled, like she was speaking underwater; her hair and clothes floated around her, too, as if suspended. She could breathe fine and wasn't wet to the touch, but her voice and hair and anything she wore didn't seem to know it.

"Not Toren, just Ento," Ento said. He didn't mind speaking here, and his voice rang like bells.

"Ento. Of course." She paused. "Where's Toren?"

Seven years dead and buried behind the family garden, but arguing with her rarely overcame the certainty of her faulty memory.

"I'm sure he'll be here soon," Ento said instead.

Gram let out a breath that sounded like bubbles. "There's some soup left in the pot there. Serve us up some."

Ento poured soup into a dish for Gram and set it on the table beside her chair.

"And some for you," she reminded him.

"Yes, Gram," he replied.

He clinked the spoon around the pot a few times to stop her worrying, then stood by the house's only window. He touched a finger to the pane and felt the coolness of the glass. Or perhaps he felt the coolness of himself against the window. Loy was so sure things would all go back to normal, which suggested things *could* go back to normal. Whether or not the magic could be scooped out of them and give them back their ordinary flesh and bone, Ento would always know what it felt like to touch glass while made of glass. The farmer's wife would always know what the Forgotten Tongue sounded like and her cat would always know the feel of a fresh kill between far too many teeth. What would the blacksmith do without his extra arms? Could the apothecary's wife forget what it was to walk on hooves?

The magic had changed them in one way, but in so doing, Ento supposed, it had changed them all in another. It had only been two weeks, but if he got his skin back and could take off those nice clothes once more, Ento was sure he'd still favor the soft grass over the rocky path and layers of leaves over cobblestones. How long would it take as his old self to again walk briskly through the market or merely curse at the pain of stumbling on a loose stone?

This had to end. Somehow, this madness had to be reversed. He thought back to Loy and the others, plotting how to see for themselves if the magic could be taken back. Life could never be normal again, but there had to be some way to get closer to it. Closer to that distant dream that was once the humdrum of ordinary things. Even with his dulled emotions, his glass heart felt it was being crushed if he did not believe that.

Except his hope was probably only that: hope. Just like the talk around the barrel had been only talk, and even if it wasn't, what could Ento do about it? Go and be shattered? He could not trust himself even on the footpath by his home. And he could not leave Gram all alone, and he might not even have the nerve for it.

Ento slid his finger against the window, ignoring the soft shriek of it as he flattened his hand against the pane. No, heroics were meant for others. He could only wait, and hope, and try not to break in the process.

"Ah, that's better to see with," Gram said as a ray of sun magnified itself through Ento's hand. "Be a dear and move over just a little."

Ento moved, and the sunbeam bathed him in golden light. Instead of a shadow upon the floor, the light magnified through his head in bright spots against the worn rug and the old wood.

"A little more light, if you could. These eyes are old," said Gram.

Ento slowly, carefully, undid the buttons of his second shirt. They *tinked* against his fingers. When he shed the faded shirt, light filled the room with orbs that made him want to shield his eyes against them and rainbows that painted what had been dark and plain. Filtered as it was through clouds and grime, he was mostly sure standing in the sun like this wouldn't cause a fire. If anything started to smolder, he'd know to make a new rule.

"That's perfect," said Gran, giving him a near-toothless grin. Her hair swayed in some invisible tide and her fingers furiously clacked her needles. "I could get used to light like this."

Elisabeth Ring *is a writer and critic living in the Western U.S. When not writing for her day job or her side hustle, she can be found running or walking with her dog, or making stodgy sourdough bread. Her work has previously appeared in Lavender Bones, and you can read her thoughts on titles from her eclectic reading list at* ringreads.com.

Untenanted

Cassandra O'Sullivan Sachar

When Hailey Abbot was six years old, she discovered she could leave her body.

Stuck at the fabric store with her mother instead of curled up on the couch watching Saturday morning cartoons with her dog, Hailey was miserable. She *hated* fabric stores, hated how her mother spent hours caressing the brightly-colored bolts beneath her finger tips.

"We'll just pop in and out," her mother would say, but then she'd start conversations about quilting techniques with ladies in the store, and Hailey would end up sitting on the dusty linoleum for hours on end, aching to leave. She didn't know what a Crazy Nine Patch pattern was and didn't care about backing versus basting—it was *so* boring.

Staring at her own open-eyed body propped against a set of shelves in the flannel section, she figured she had fallen asleep.

But Hailey could see everything around her clearly—it wasn't like her regular dreams, where objects looked fuzzy, as if she were wearing swimming goggles. She even noticed a fleck of dried ketchup on her other self's chin. When she rubbed her own face, she felt the dry, flaky texture.

It seemed wrong, somehow, seeing herself this way. She searched for her mother at the back of the store, still chatting away.

Hailey knew she wasn't supposed to interrupt when grownups were talking, but she did it anyway, wanting the creepy feeling to go away. "Are you almost done, Mom?"

But her mother kept talking like she wasn't even there. Hailey reached for her sleeve but watched her fingers slither right through.

Her chest tightened, as if she were underwater and needed to come up for air. She felt a pulling sensation, a frantic tug to her other self. Hailey allowed herself to be dragged back to the flannel section and poured into her body like pancake batter onto a griddle.

She opened and closed her fist, making sure both selves were together as one. "Mom?"

Her voice, loud and quivering, must have indicated her distress, for Hailey's mother rushed to her side. Crouching on her knees, frowning, she felt Hailey's forehead. "Are you okay, honey? You look pale."

Hailey was a good girl who tried to tell the truth. But when she opened her mouth, all she said was, "I think I need to eat something."

On the car ride home, belly full of ice cream, Hailey thought about what had happened and decided she couldn't tell, even though it scared her. *Especially* because it scared her.

The next time Hailey left her body, she was in third grade, taking an oral spelling test and trying to picture the word "homonym." Her teacher, Miss Goldstein, had a poster behind her desk with that word written on it, but Hailey couldn't see it in her mind's eye.

Then there she was, staring at it.

Hailey flushed red, waiting for the teacher's reprimand for getting up during a test and cheating, but Miss Goldstein simply gave the next word, "repetition." Hailey's other self sat at her desk, unmoving, not writing a word.

She didn't want Miss Goldstein to notice. She rushed back into her body and resumed her exam.

By middle school, Hailey had learned some control. Though she still slipped out of her body accidentally at times, often when distracted or upset, she could now leave at will. But she remained careful.

Once, she had gone wandering—for that's what she called it—while watching television with her mother. She knew no one could see or hear her, and she had built up endurance to go for longer times and farther distances from her body. She passed through the door and glided down the street, moving lighter and more gracefully than when in her body.

She watched the late summer sunset, appreciating the creamy sherbet colors bleeding into each other, before heading back inside.

But when she reentered the house, her mother's screams filled the room. She jumped back into her body.

"Mom! Stop! What are you doing?" Hailey wrenched her mother's arms away.

"Hailey! I thought you were dead! I called 9-1-1!" Her mother spoke into the phone: "She's okay—I don't know what happened. Yes, yes, I will follow up with the doctor."

"I'm fine. I must've fallen asleep."

"Your eyes were open. They were about to have me do mouth to mouth!" With her mother's face a tearstained mask of anguish, Hailey's guilt consumed her.

From then on, she limited her wandering—she'd only leave from her room with the door locked and music playing. If her mother knocked on the door, she'd have a few minutes' leeway to say she hadn't heard her, an interlude to do whatever she wanted with no one the wiser.

Hailey's power enthralled her. Sashaying outside in the dead of winter in her pajamas, she didn't feel cold when wandering and left no footsteps in snow. Nighttime was best, for her mother was less prone to check on her, and Hailey adored watching the nocturnal creatures: the deer, guileless to any presence, munching away on the grass while the wolf stayed in the shadows under the moonlit sky, waiting for the opportunity to begin the hunt. Only Hailey, undetected, could view nature's majesty this way.

She stayed away longer and longer, heading back when her lungs started begging for air and the tide pulled her back to her body.

Hailey wondered if there were some great purpose as to why she could come and go as she pleased, a reason she could shed her flesh like a winter coat, but she had no insight and no one to talk to. Her wandering was just something she could do, like how some people could wiggle

their ears. She gave up questioning and focused on enjoying her secret.

Until she was caught.

The Russos lived a few doors down from the Abbots' house. Hailey wasn't really listening when her mother told her about the elder Mrs. Russo moving in. Hailey had babysat for the family a few times, but little Charlie threw terrible tantrums, so she pretended to be busy unless in dire need of cash.

As Hailey sailed through the neighborhood over a sea of fallen leaves one autumn evening, the old lady standing on the lawn seemed to look straight at her. By now, Hailey was accustomed to this discomfort—she didn't bat an eyelid.

"I see you, Hailey Abbot," Mrs. Russo's voice, full of gravel and razor blades, reverberated out to her.

Hailey slid to a halt. How did this woman know her name? Better yet, how could she *see* her?

"You can see me? Can you *hear* me?" Hailey approached with caution; she couldn't believe it, not after all of these years going unnoticed.

"Clear as daylight. Better than my ruined eyes can see from my actual body." She gestured toward the house with her thumb. "I'm inside, lying in my hospital bed. Now that I can't walk, can't do anything, really, I like getting outside for a change of scenery and to pretend I can breathe this fresh air. Meanwhile, my earthly lungs are chock full of fluid."

Hailey gaped at her. There was so much to ask; she wanted to feast on the old woman's wisdom like it was a big, thick steak.

"Cat got your tongue, girl? If you've got something to say, out with it. I don't know how much longer I have."

Hailey didn't know if Mrs. Russo meant she'd need to go back to her body soon, or if she was suggesting that she was dying. She didn't want to be insensitive, but she wanted more information from this single person who could understand her gift. "You wander, Mrs. Russo?"

"Ever since I was a girl. But I call it traveling. And call me Agnes." She smiled, eyes gleaming. "You?"

"Since I was six." Hailey started blurting it all out to this stranger, spilling the secrets she had kept, from the first time in the fabric store to her longer and more recent trips, nearly twelve years later. She said so much so fast that she almost didn't notice the familiar feeling, the constricted lungs and wrenching back to her body.

Agnes knew. Of course she did. "Young lady, this has been a pleasant gab session, but I can tell you need to go. Tomorrow, same time, same place?"

Hailey nodded, regretting how she had monopolized their conversation, wishing she had asked Agnes about her own experiences.

They met the next day, and the next, and Hailey remembered to listen rather than share. Agnes understood Hailey's need for guidance.

"Look, sister, I'll tell you what I know. I've been traveling for seventy-odd years, but the doctor says my days are numbered. Somebody might as well benefit from all this knowledge. If that person is you, and I can help you, great."

Agnes told her stories about leaving her body for hours on end, giving Hailey tips on building up strength so she could do it, too. She regaled Hailey with tales of going backstage with the Beatles and standing by as Queen Elizabeth ate her dinner.

"I had to haul my earthly body to England first, but the sky's the limit once you park your carcass near Buckingham Palace. I boogied right past those guards with their big, silly hats. I had a ball." Agnes sighed, a small smile playing on her lips. "What I wouldn't give to be in your shoes now, ready to start your journey."

Alive with possibility, Hailey planned events in her future. As soon as she graduated high school next month, before she started college, she could do whatever she liked. Harry Styles! Beyoncé! What great fun it would be, enjoying life in a way almost no one else could. Following Agnes's example, she could go anywhere, do anything: walk through every velvet rope, slide down Niagara Falls or the Grand Canyon.

One day, at their normal meeting time, Agnes wasn't waiting for her.

Panic coursed through Hailey's veins. Had she passed? Agnes had said she wasn't long for this world.

Hailey didn't want to intrude, but she peeked into the Russos' house to check if her friend was okay. There lay Agnes in the hospital bed, looking so much weaker and smaller than how Hailey knew her. Her eyes, cloudy with glaucoma, were open, but Hailey knew her friend was still alive—the machine at her bedside registered a weak heartbeat.

If Agnes was out wandering, where had she gone? She was always there for Hailey. They were there for each other, the only two people who understood this special talent.

Hailey left the Russos' and searched the neighborhood. Maybe Agnes was out on a nature walk. But she couldn't find her anywhere.

Her chest burning, Hailey headed home, saddened by the lack of connection. She passed through her front door and into her bedroom, anxious to get back into her body.

But her body was no longer lying in bed. Instead, Hailey gasped in horror to see herself sitting at her desk, laptop open to a travel site, singing along with Spotify to "Hey, Jude."

Hailey tried to climb back into this moving, blinking being, *her* body, but there was no room. Though her lungs gulped for air, Hailey realized she wasn't feeling the gravitational tug to come back to her body.

Instead, she was pulled away, in another direction. Weak with betrayal, she let the current drag her in—she knew where she was headed. She just needed to breathe, and she'd come back to claim what was rightfully hers. *Her* body. *Her* life.

Down the street she soared, through the front door of the Russos' house.

She had no choice. She climbed into the atrophied figure stretched out on the bed, desperate to release the pressure in her lungs.

Hailey waited for everything to come into focus, like it normally did when she came back to her body, but the eyes through which she stared stayed foggy, and the pressure in her lungs hadn't abated—if anything, it had grown, and she took deep, gasping breaths, unable to escape the vice clamping her chest.

"Help me," she croaked.

Mr. Russo rushed in and grasped her hand, a shriveled, veiny claw.

"Mom, I'm here. The doctor said it won't be long now. You'll be at peace."

Hot tears leaked out of eyes that were not hers, and the thin chest that was not Hailey's moved up and down, up and down, and finally stopped.

Cassandra O'Sullivan Sachar is a writer and associate English professor in Pennsylvania. Her creative work has appeared or is forthcoming in over twenty literary journals, magazines, and anthologies including the horror publications Ink Stains: A Dark Fiction Literary Anthology, The Horror Zine, Eerie Christmas 2, 666: Dark Drabbles, Tales from the Moonlit Path, and Black Petals Horror/Science Fiction Magazine. She holds a Doctorate of Education with a Literacy Specialization from the University of Delaware and is working toward an MFA in Creative Writing at Wilkes University. Additionally, she is the current fiction editor at River and South Review.

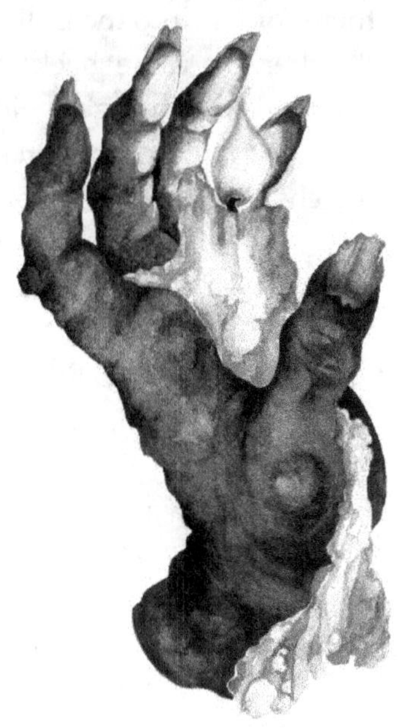

Hanna's Journey

by Tom Jolly

I don't remember being torn from my master's body, if, indeed, that's how I came to be. Birth is never more than a shadow of a memory, an indistinct feeling of presence, even for a disembodied hand. Like me.

I could sense my surroundings in detail, even though I had no eyes. The man looming over me, staring into the little holly box I called home, was young, with wavy black hair and a struggling wisp of a beard. His black hoody, damp from the fog outside, was pulled back. The dim store lights brightened my day with flickering fluorescence.

"It looks real," he said.

"It was a movie prop," the store owner replied. "If it were real, the hand would be all shriveled and black. I've seen real ones," he bragged. The store was a small novelty and junk shop, though the owner carried a variety of pseudo-occult paraphernalia: scented candles, crystals, mystical pendants, sachets of potpourri, homemade brooms and such. Not really the sort of thing magicians used.

The potential customer lifted the box to his nose and sniffed. I tried to lie very still. There was no easy way out of the shop, and I desperately wanted to return to my master. If this man purchased me, I'd have a way out. The shop owner tended to keep the latch thrown on the box, severely limiting my freedom of movement. The one time he left it open, I got out and crawled around the shop, searching for an exit.

That brief evening of freedom exploring the shop showed me that there was no gap large enough for a wizard's hand to slip through. Having failed to find an escape, I crawled up the side of a wicker basket and climbed back into my holly box, nestled amongst the cedar shavings, my little bed. I used one finger to close the lid.

Today was another day. The young man flipped me out of the box into his own hand. It was hard remaining still, but I had to if I ever wanted to leave that stupid little shop. "Feels papery," he said. No surprise, I thought. I had been detached from my master for years. Over a hundred, but I wasn't sure of the exact count. The curse that tore my immortal master apart before his bits were sent to the far corners of the Earth happened so long ago that I lost track of time. But dry and papery? Give me a little hand lotion and I'd be good as new.

The guy returned me to the box and carried me to the cash register. Yes! I was about to be free, after a fashion. To reach this point, after my master was defeated, I'd been locked in a tomb, then discovered by a team of looters who sold me at a bazaar of the bizarre to the owner of a circus freak show. Then the circus shut down or faded away and the liquidation of their assets put me in a large lot that the curio shop bought, and then Max, the current shop owner, slapped a high price on me and put me on display. He got a kick out of the reaction from startled customers.

I might have been the only legitimately magical item in the entire store. But Max wouldn't know that. I'd learned to stay very still. If I had moved, then I would become a curiosity that would never be free. A prized possession. And I'd never find my master.

He was somewhere to the northeast. Maybe a mile, maybe a thousand. All I had was a vague feeling which direction I needed to go. I assumed that his feet, legs, arms, and torso had that same feeling, but for the life of me, I had no idea how they would get there. At least I could crawl. What would someone make of a torso stashed away somewhere, anyway? What would they do with it if found? Bury it? Would it have to squirm up from the depths and wriggle toward the master's head like some giant pink slug?

Brendan Colewell, the man who purchased me, tossed my box into the back of his Honda Civic and drove me to his small house in Santa Maria. I wondered what he did for a living, but it became irrelevant when he brought me to a room that was clearly meant for nothing but real magic. There was no carpet at all, only a cement slab with two pentagrams embedded in it, both made of copper. Three shelves held a variety of ingredients, paraphernalia, and old books, and there was a small wooden desk with a laptop computer on it.

He opened the box and stared hard at me for a minute, then picked me up and examined me more closely, rubbing the blond hairs on the back of my fingers and tugging on them. Making faces. Examining the end of the stump where there used to be an arm attached, with a nub of bright white bone jutting from the wrist. "Well," he said, "who did you once belong to?"

So, apparently he thought I was real. Bonus points for the kid. He scratched his head and turned to his computer, opening some occult research page, and entered, "historical dismembered hands" and surprisingly got a good number of results. A lot of them referenced the hands of saints; apparently carrying around a finger-joint from a saint was supposed to be a good thing. And there was "The Hand of Glory," cut from a hanged man, which had its own odd magic. But there was nothing about me. I wasn't surprised. If my master had minions who were searching for his parts after his dismemberment, then those who had performed the act of destroying him would certainly want the location of his parts to remain secret for as long as possible. Preferably forever.

Brendan called up a genealogy website, locating one that could derive useful data from skin cells, and ordered a sample kit. I had to admit, this had never occurred to me. Would my master appear on some genealogy chart, with "occupation: evil wizard" filled in? Would there be some grainy tintype copied onto the internet with his scowling face glaring out at us? Or did he exist before photography?

I hoped to have crawled away by the time the DNA kit arrived and avoid the mild indignity of having some of my cells scraped away. But glancing around the room, I saw that the only means of egress were a ceiling vent and the door. There were no windows, which didn't surprise me. I made a wild guess that the door to the room was always locked since anyone practicing real magic wasn't going to want anybody accidentally stumbling across their activities. As for the ceiling vent; well, it was attached to the ceiling, and I couldn't fly, so that was useless.

He returned his attention to me. "What *is* your story?" he asked, picking me up and turning me over. He ran a finger along my lifeline, as if that could tell him something. Putting me back down, he pulled a cellphone out of his back pocket and dialed. "Hi, Maggot," he said. "You wouldn't believe what I found. No, not that. Yeah, kiss my ass. It's an actual hand. Yep. I didn't even have to kill anyone for it. In a thrift shop, well, you know that wannabe occult store? That one. Uh-huh. He thought it was fake. So you know that 'finder' spell that required a dismembered hand that we discussed?" He looked at me again and grinned. "I think we have the materials for it now."

I was to become an ensorcelled artifact. Something that found things, pointed the way to them. I wondered if that would help me locate the rest of my immortal master's parts? But it might not matter; his body parts all knew where they had to go. It was just a matter of getting past the barriers that chance threw in our way. Once I was out in the wild, it would be easy enough to crawl through the brush at night and hide under the leaves and dirt during the day, for however many miles it might take to reach him.

Brendan made a shopping list, because, in fact, he didn't really have all the ingredients that he thought he did. He left the room and locked the door from the outside, but I could see the knob from the deadbolt turn from the inside. If I could reach it, I could leave.

After I heard the front door of the house open and close and the Honda drive away, I jumped off the tabletop onto the chair, then down to the floor. Practically, it's hard to climb up a table leg to get onto the top of a table, but I could jump about a foot by pointing my wrist in the air, knuckling my fingers, then flinging them wide. As long as the surfaces were close, like the seat and tabletop, I could move fairly fast.

The chair was relatively light, so I wrapped two fingers around one leg and dragged it across the floor, across one of the copper pentagrams, and leaned the back of the chair against the doorknob. Jumping onto the seat and climbing the back of the chair, I opened the deadbolt. Then I pushed a finger against the frame of door while rotating the knob and, voila! The door inched open, pushing the chair with it.

I jumped down to the floor and wedged myself into the small gap. So close to freedom, though it would only be the start of my journey to find my master! I wriggled through into Brendan's living room.

The front door was also locked, of course. A kitchenette held a small, cheap dining table with two wooden chairs that appeared to be small enough for me to move, but there was a throw rug between the chairs and the door that would slow me down. Do-able, though. I pulled the carpet back to expose the bare wooden floor, and then I heard the stupid car pull up. It was far too soon for him to have done his shopping. I knew he had to visit at least two stores; he said

as much.

On the other hand, this might be a great opportunity. Luck doesn't make itself. I ran over to the door.

I heard the key in the lock and stood on tense fingertips right next to the door frame, and as soon as the door swung open, I scrambled for freedom, hoping that he didn't glance down.

He did. "What the…" he jerked back away from me, his eyes panning along with my rapid digiperambulation as I scurried for the local shrubbery. He was stunned motionless.

Boris was not. Boris, a huge, orange tomcat that I had to assume was regularly fed a diet of wriggling human body parts, pounced on me delightedly as I passed by him and gleefully wrestled with me as I tried to escape from his painfully clawed grasp.

Brendan sauntered over to view the carnage from a closer perspective. "Hey Boris, what did you find for me? Not a gopher head this time, huh?" He bent over and petted the huge beast who purred loudly while somehow keeping me in a feline full Nelson.

He grabbed my wrist and slowly disengaged me from its velociraptor-like claws and held me up to get a good look, and said, "Well, well. You've been holding out on me, my friend." I snapped my fingers just to give him a start and was satisfied when he jumped. Then he turned and walked back into my new prison: his house.

He let bloody Boris into his living room, petting it a few more times to show how appreciative he was, then walked back into his den, nodding as he admired my skill at accessing the door.

"Smart, too, I see," he said. "You can plan. So where were you going then?"

He closed and locked the door again and scooted the chair back over to his desk, then placed me on top. I wondered if I could jump up and strangle him, but that was something I had never tried. And frankly, I was curious where this was going. Other humans who'd seen me turned and ran, screaming. Brendan appeared to find me anomalous and interesting.

He stared at me for a minute. I rolled my fingers, as though impatient, which made him chuckle. Finally, he scooted his computer keyboard over to face me. There was a blank white page displayed on the screen.

"You speak English?" he asked.

My fingers twitched in the air, momentarily surprised. But then I turned to the keyboard and pecked "Yes."

"Where were you going in such a hurry?"

That seemed a particularly poignant question, considering all the questions I expected, like, "How is it that you're alive?" and so on. But this one question would answer most of the others he might have. I debated on whether to tell him anything useful, but it occurred to me that I could use him to find my master. He might even take me there, bypassing the cats and dogs and birds and other pests that might otherwise slow me down. And my master would be able to give him something he wanted: magic.

I typed, "I wish to return to my main body, the magician Louis de la Croix. He will reward you grandly."

He rubbed his chin thoughtfully, staring at the words on the screen. "That name sounds a little familiar," he said. "Excuse me for a sec." He picked me up and moved me to the side, then ran a search on the occult research site that he'd accessed earlier. He found a short history under, "Magicians, myths, circa 1700." He looked back at me and I lifted my thumb and pinky to simulate an open-handed shrug. He seemed to get it. "Louis de la Croix was a sorcerer in the New Orleans area," he read out loud, presumably for my sake, unaware that though I lacked eyes, I could see just fine (something I have never understood, really. Skin can detect heat, so perhaps that has something to do with it).

He continued, "The myth surrounded the man is that he sacrificed a small town of seventy-six people, Ville des Âmes, to acquire immortality, and where the town used to be is now a large sinkhole. Three witches in the area banded together to paralyze him and then cut him up into living pieces, since his immortality extended beyond his dismemberment. While they first meant to burn the pieces to finish the job, the head seemed to encourage and welcome the burning, complaining about the horror of being kept alive forever, yet separate. This theme of reverse psychology arises in many American stories, such as Br'er Rabbit and the Briar Patch, or with Tom Sawyer whitewashing the fence, and might be discounted as fiction itself."

He returned to gaze at me and asked, "Is that how it was? Your wizard tricked the witches into keeping him alive?"

I shrugged again. But it was true. He

tricked them more eloquently and deviously than this simple history could describe, and the witches were convinced that they were punishing him most severely by keeping him alive and separated into pieces, forever. But he knew better, and that the pieces, no matter how remote, would always attract each other, and if it took a hundred or a thousand years, he would become whole again, somehow.

I wondered where Louis' head was and what it was doing right then.

"So how do we find the other parts of your Louis?" Brendan asked.

I stood on four digits and pointed northeast with my index finger, then typed, "I can sense him."

"And you say he would reward us to take you to him?"

I bobbed up and down.

"Hmm. And he really killed seventy-six people to make himself immortal?"

This felt like a trick question. I mean, sure, I was there. My digits helped cast the soul-sucking spell, thus making my master immortal, so yeah, he did that thing. But it seemed to dampen the "reward" scenario a little if Brendan thought that Louis was a psychopath. I typed, "He will reward you greatly," again, giving the carrot a little shake.

"Uh-huh," he said. His voice didn't carry the conviction of a devoted minion.

Someone rapped on the front door. "That's probably Maggot," he said, and stood up. As he opened the door to his room, I saw Boris' eyes framed by orange fur, staring hungrily into the room. Brendan shoved the cat out of the way with his foot and closed the door,

leaving me alone.

I heard the front door open and close and then their voices, muffled somewhat by the door between us. There were a few obvious exclamations that came through clearly: "Alive?" And "It's intelligent?" And "you talked to the hand?" Then, "Let me see it!"

There was a pause and Brendan lowered his voice a lot. I caught, "black magic," and "murdered" mixed into the conversation, with Maggot responding with "blah, blah, learn a lot."

Then they went outside where I couldn't hear them and continued talking, returning a few minutes later.

Maggot was enthralled with my existence. "Wow, a crawling hand!" I gave him a thumbs-up and he just about fell over.

"We have a proposition for you, hand," Brendan said.

"Let's call him Hans," Maggot suggested.

Brendan chuckled. "There's only one. Maybe just 'Han'?"

"Han solo!" He shouted, laughing.

I didn't see what was so funny, but they started calling me Han from then on. I'd never had a name before. Self-identity. How could I? I was a small part of a whole, part of something greater and more important than myself.

"Have you ever thought about going it alone?" Brendan asked me. "Being your own man, so to speak? Just leaving your master handless?"

I typed "No. I feel a strong urge to return to my master."

The two of them looked knowingly at each other, and Brendan asked, "Is it a strong urge, or do you actually *want* to go back to Louis de la Croix?

Well, that was nuanced. An urge or a desire? "What's the difference?" I typed.

"Think of a drug," Maggot suggested. "You might have an urge to take it, but deep down, you don't want to be addicted to it and want to resist."

I considered that explanation and examined my inner thoughts and feelings. It was more urge than anything. Though being back with the rest of myself was appealing on its own. But I typed "urge".

"Okay. So you might be under a geas of some sort, forcing you to go back to Louis. We have the tools here to lift a geas. Let us do that, and if you still want to return to Louis afterward, we'll take you there. But we're hoping you'll just hang out here with us."

Hang out? I turned back and forth to take in their hopeful faces. Why would they want me here? To feed the cat? I remembered that he wanted me as a component in a 'finder' spell, pretty basic stuff. I supposed it wouldn't hurt, and at the least, I'd be on a fast-track to reach my master.

They prepared one of the two pentagrams with candles and chalk symbols and placed me in the center (I could have walked there, but they didn't even give me the option—I'm not lazy). They lit the candles, said some words, and waved their hands in complicated patterns, and the geas lifted from me in a swirl of blue fog. They were stunned that there was a visible component in the execution of the spell and rushed to turn on the ceiling vent to clear out the magic fog. If I had a mouth, I would have laughed.

They put me back on the desk. "How do you feel now? Urge gone?"

I bobbed up and down, though there was some desire remaining. It just seemed natural.

"The urge is gone. But I still wish to go to my master," I typed.

Brendan seemed disappointed. "You know, if you recombine with your master, you won't actually think anymore. You'll just be another piece of his body, just his..." He stopped and glanced at his own hands, then at me, then finished, "...right hand. Though you'll still be alive, you might as well be dead. No thoughts of your own, *nada*."

Well, I *was* just a hand. I was my master's hand. I would never have existed without him. I belonged there. I couldn't let my own self interfere with that decision.

I typed, "You agreed to take me to my master."

Brendan sighed. "So we did," he said.

And that was that.

I was in a shoebox in the back seat of Brendan's Honda Civic. The rear windows were tinted, allowing me to peer out whenever I wanted to without being seen, but the view going through Bakersfield wasn't much to talk about. Not that I had any reference for what was pretty and what wasn't. Most of my experience with scenery was limited to the inside walls of a variety of containers. I could, at least, offer an educated critique on the esthetic appeal of beeswax finishes over varnish.

We hit State Route 58 going east and stopped at one of the infrequent gas stations tucked alongside the road.

Brendan gassed up and told me to stay in the car since he didn't 'need a hand'. Then he laughed. Speaking of urges, I wanted to slap him around a little just then.

Maggot went inside to load up on snacks and came back with two bags of chips, two candy bars, and sodas. He leaned into the car to deposit his treasure and then glanced back at me, hoisted up on the side of my cardboard box. "Oh, hey, I forgot. Did you want something?"

Side effect of immortality; I didn't have to eat. For someone without a mouth, that was very fortunate. I waggled a 'no'.

Maggot said, "Hey, I saw something inside you might like. In a gumball machine. Couldn't resist." He pulled two plastic rings out of his pocket. Each one had a googly-eye attached to it. For some dumb reason, I got all excited and held out my index and forefingers and he slid them on. They were a little loose; Louis had slender fingers. I waggled my fingers with a simple 'fitting' cantrip and the rings snugged up on my fingers. Maggot tried to get Brendan's attention and while his back was turned, I layered on another cantrip for moving very light objects, and the small black beads in my white plastic eyes became my tools. There wasn't much magic a wizard could do with one hand, and I was pleased with myself for even thinking of it.

Brendan stuck his head in the car and my eyes moved to stare at him. I could see him fine before, but now he could see me seeing him. "Holy crap! They sell magic rings here?"

"Magic?" Maggot leaned in to look. I rolled my eyes at him because I could. "Wow, that is awesome," he said.

And it was. I loved that I had googly-eyes. I could stare at people and make them nervous, if being a disembodied crawling hand wasn't enough.

We drove and drove, passing through Las Vegas and an other-worldly canyon filled with huge black rocks that loomed over us, as though they were going to fall on us at any second. We made it most of the way through Utah before a highway patrolman pulled us over. After writing Brendan a ticket for going five miles an hour too fast, he happened to see the box in the back seat. My box. "What you boys got in the box?" He sniffed. "Is that weed I smell?" The lid was on, so I couldn't really see what transpired between the police officer and the boys, but they ended up behind our car with a second cop rummaging through the car. He grabbed the box, and I heard some low-level spell mumbled from Brendan, and the cop opened it and stared down at my googly-eyes. I didn't budge.

"What is it?" The first cop said.

"A pair of shoes. In a shoebox," the second cop replied.

The boys did good. I didn't really want to wind up stuck in an evidence locker.

They let us go with the ticket, and off we went.

I wanted to compliment them on the spell they cast, even if it was a minor one, since it facilitated my mission. I crawled up front and tapped on Maggot's cell phone where it was plugged into the charger. We'd tested this system before; one of them could put the phone in a "notes" mode and I could type on the tiny keyboard. It wasn't easy and I made a few mistakes, but I knew where the backspace was.

"Kind of a shame," Maggot said while I tapped away in the back of the car, "we could get you an email account, Facebook account, Twitter account, and you could talk to anyone. But you'll be dead in a few days, so why bother?"

I stopped typing. Not dead, I thought, but part of a larger, better organism. My body. The rest of me. Of course, the 'rest of me' wouldn't remember this trip, or Maggot, or the googly-eyes. I drooped a little.

Maggot took the phone from me, thinking that I was finished. "You guys," he read, "performed Vanmore's Distorted Attention very well. I think…" He twisted around to look at me. "You think what?"

I thought they had great potential as sorcerers. Sure, they'd complained about the moral issues of allowing Louis to reassemble himself, and how he'd sacrificed so many people to achieve immortality, but didn't all sorcerers do that eventually? They would age, their time would come, and they'd have to make that same decision.

"Hey," Maggot said. "We can download this app that turns your typing into speech. You can actually talk to us."

Magic still exists, I thought. Humans just refer to it as "technology," fooling themselves into thinking that there's nothing supernatural about it. My master can make a book read itself aloud. These modern wizards can give me a voice. And eyes, of a sort.

Maggot downloaded the 'app' and activated it, then slid the phone back to me. "You said that spell that Brendan cast was called what?" he asked.

"Vanmore's Distorted Attention." I had a strangely metallic voice. The two of them laughed at it, though I had no idea why. "The spell is over two hundred years old," I continued. "Lord Vanmore created or discovered it, and was killed later by Jome Hazelwort with a Corley's Unequal Shrinking."

"How do you know all this stuff?" Brendan asked. "When you were separated from Louis, didn't your memories start from nothing?"

"No," I typed. "My master duplicated much of his knowledge among his parts so that they could defend themselves. I know many small spells, but I am limited to those without audible components or the use of the left hand."

They were still chuckling at the sound of my voice. "What is wrong with my voice? It sounds strange."

"It's just a famous guy," Maggot said. "You wouldn't know him. You want a different voice?"

"Yes," I said.

"Male or female?"

My master was male. My choice was obvious. But I hesitated. I had a voice. I had memories. I had a name. It would all disappear soon. I wasn't my master; I was different. "Female," I said.

They both glanced back at me, then faced forward. "We've got a selection," Maggot said.

I don't know if they suggested it as a joke, or if I saw some ad while playing around with Maggot's phone, but around Denver, cruising down the I-70, we decided I needed fingernail polish. Finding a salon willing to put fingernail polish on a disembodied hand was going to be difficult, so we just decided to magic our way through it. Maggot, wearing a loose jacket, grabbed me by the wrist and pulled his arm into his sleeve to make it appear that I was really his own hand. It looked like a setup for a cheesy cheap magic trick, except that I could move.

He walked into the parlor and got some odd looks, but they took him in, and we cast another Vanmore's to make sure everything at least appeared normal. Maggot got my nails done on his right side, and his own nails done on the left. Mine were white with little dragon figures in the center of each one. Being immortal and regenerating constantly, my nails were perfect. Our manicurist described them as immaculate.

On our way out, the manicurist, calm as could be, said to Maggot, "You know that cantrip shit doesn't work on Wiccans."

And Maggot said, "Uh." He glanced down to take in her pentacle pendant. "Yeah, I should have noticed."

"Most guys notice right away," she said. She dipped her head at me. "Take care of your little friend there, but be careful. That is some nasty magic you're screwing with."

They nodded solemnly and I waved at her, which made her smile and frown all at once. "I like the eyes, by the way," she added. "Nice touch."

When we got to the car, I signaled to use the voice app and said, "Hanna, not Han."

They nodded together. "Pleased to make your acquaintance, Hanna," Brendan said, and started the car. I did a little dance there on the back seat, and have no idea what they thought of that and didn't really care.

Out of Denver, we left the I-70 and headed up I-80, still generally northeast, until we got to Gothenburg, Nebraska. From there, my sense of direction took us north and down a bumpy dirt road under a canopy of heavy branches to an abandoned graveyard. I clung to the edge of the window, staring outside, not knowing what to expect.

They parked on a bare patch of grass next to the graveyard. There were a few plots surrounded by rusty steel fences and a few with tall monuments declaring the importance of their contents, if anyone happened by to read them. A couple of large family crypts with doors and locks loomed over the back of the graveyard like ominous guardians.

"You know you can still kiss this off, Hanna," Brendan said yet again. "You don't have to be part of a whole when you can be a piece of yourself."

I looked at my bright nails with my googly-eyes (though the plastic eyes weren't actually seeing anything) and thought about how much this would irritate the sorcerer Louis de la Croix. I typed, "I should tell him that I…" and then the phone died and the engine died and there we sat. My unfinished words: …that I want to split from him. I'd never considered that possibility, not for a few hundred years of riding around in small boxes, until these two decided to bring it up. Like it was perfectly natural, a hand living on its own. I'd had a few days to think about it, taste it, see what I thought about it. And frankly, having a couple of supportive friends made a huge difference.

"Oh boy," Maggot said.

The two of them got out of the car. I rode on Brendan's shoulder to stay out of the tall grass. A door to one of the family crypts creaked opened, and a thing stepped out.

I recognized the face easy enough, kind of wobbly on the assortment of limbs supporting it. It was Louis. My master. But the geas was gone. The urge departed. The desire waning.

Not every bodily component had returned to him. Perhaps the torso had been buried by some well-meaning person and had been unable to wriggle its way back to its master. I can't imagine what someone would think if they spotted a hundred-pound worm crawling across the countryside. As a result, what we encountered was two legs, one a stump and the other connected to a foot, and one arm with a hand attached. The brainless, thoughtless, subdued left hand. The one that wasn't me.

The limbs and the head were all connected with a twisted knot of flesh, like a giant corrupted bug with some of its legs pulled off. Its three-limbed movement was awkward, and before it got close to us, it said, "Give me my hand."

The boys glanced at one another, then Brendan said, "There was supposed to be some reward?"

"And what gave you that idea?" De

la Croix said.

They both pointed at me, and I waved at my ex-master.

"My hand told you this?"

They nodded.

De la Croix's mouth worked as though he were chewing something distasteful, then he said, "I can sense that you are also practitioners of the arts. For your reward, I will allow you to be my servants. Perhaps you will learn enough to become apprentices, over time."

I slithered down to the ground and pulled on Brendan's pants leg, toward the car. He glanced down at me. I pointed toward the car. He sighed and said, "You couldn't have made this decision, like, ten miles ago?"

"My hand?" De la Croix repeated. He moved closer, his limbs flopping forward grotesquely. "Give it to me."

Brendan spread his hands apologetically and said, "Sorry Lou, old buddy, but it looks like Hanna wants to come with us."

De la Croix seemed ready to explode. He started a complex curling and stretching of the digits of his left hand and mouthed some ancient words, but he wasn't near as powerful as before. There were some spells that just required both hands to execute. Still, it sounded like the beginning of a paralysis spell, which in his skilled hands—I mean hand—could stop a heart, too.

Maggot stepped forward with a small red cylinder in his hand, raised it, and sprayed de la Croix full in the face. Some mysterious modern magic, right in his open mouth and eyes. De la Croix screamed and howled and writhed in pain, and even I felt my skin burn from the tiny bit of the toxic cloud that touched me. But de la Croix had amazing willpower; he blinked several times, spat repeatedly, and started again, his voice ragged from the strange chemicals.

Brendan pulled a handkerchief out of his back pocket and shoved it in de la Croix's mouth to keep him from talking, then grabbed the twitching, curling hand with the red vapors swirling around it, but de la Croix started kicking the heck out of him. Since he was mostly legs anyway, this was surprisingly effective.

I wanted to shout: Hey, guys, use your magic! You're magicians! But they seemed to be doing okay with mundane items. Some magicians did slow magic and weren't suited for combat. They might spend a couple of days transmuting an object in a pentagram but have no clue how to pull off the one-second double-hand actions needed to get a fireball off.

But this was the same problem de la Croix was having. Paralysis was a decent one-handed spell, but it took almost five seconds to cast.

De la Croix simply spit the rag out of his mouth while trying to kick Brendan off. Maggot was running for the car, picking out a key as he ran. He stumbled, recovered, and unlocked the trunk.

Brendan finally lost his grip on de la Croix, and I was so engrossed with the fight that I didn't notice that the fight had come to me, just a few yards away. I heard de la Croix voice some simple spell, something he hadn't given to me when we split up. Then he kicked once

more and flung Brendan away with more strength than a patchwork human should have, and I tried to scurry out of reach. Two leaps and he was upon me, sweeping me up with his other hand. He stood triumphantly on his leg and stump, held me high in the air, and said, "Ha, ha!" gloatingly. A half-second from securing me to the knot of flesh collecting the rest of his bits together.

All I could think of at that moment, that fraction of a second, is how goofy I'd look sticking out of that clump. That, and the imminent demise of my hard-earned sense of self.

An uncapped gas can, cartwheeling ropes of gasoline into the air, smacked me out of his grip. I fell into the grass, stunned and smelling of gasoline, and de la Croix fell backward. I became aware that I had, in fact, heard an aiming cantrip from Maggot. Good for him!

Both of my boys spit out the simplest of beginner spells; ignite.

I caught on fire and de la Croix burst into flames, at least where the gasoline had touched upon him, but it was enough. He was rolling around in the grass, his old parchment-dry, gasoline-soaked skin burning, and he might have quenched it with a spell if Maggot hadn't dashed forward, grabbed the gas can, and poured the rest on his flailing limbs.

I felt a heavy mass land on me, smothering me, smothering the flames, and blocking my googly sight. Brendan had saved me.

"Just think if we'd had a gun," Maggot said.

"Wouldn't have helped," I said with my nifty new phone. I can only describe my current voice as sultry. "The immortality was proof against everything but flames. He survived after having his head cut off for two hundred years. Why do you think a bullet would have made a difference?"

I was resting on my usual pillow, scratching Boris' ears. I don't think he'd quite figured out what to make of me, but as long as the ear-scratching continued, we were good.

"We got lucky," Brendan said. "Guessing that fire would work from that article about the witches was the first bit of dumb luck. And why wasn't he more powerful? An ancient immortal?"

"Much of his power was used to maintain his body," I said. "He couldn't eat—he had no stomach. It was only magic keeping him alive. And that lowered his power. Plus, he was missing his right-hand man."

"Cute," Maggot said.

Together, we constituted the Wizards of Hollow Oak Lane, where Brendan's house was located. They specialized in copy spells and transmutation spells, which is where the two pentagrams came into play. Their initial goal had been to copy hundred dollar bills or diamonds, but the rules of magic seemed to parallel some thermodynamic rules in a peculiar way; you couldn't get more out of a system than you put into it. Thus, components required for a copy or transmutation always ended up costing more than the end result was worth. We were studying exactly why magic would pay any attention at all to the economic value of an item, but it did, even when those values changed.

The boys finally had their opportunity to create a 'finding' talisman, that is, a dead-man's hand with a spell on it. I could find any lost item easily, and that was our real bread-and-butter. It was so much simpler to find a lost diamond ring for someone else and get paid for it than it was to copy one with magic.

They used a prop (me) to impress the customers. I just had to remember to stay as still as possible until the reveal, and then I got to twitch. Man, the look on their faces.

I like it here. I don't know how I'll feel in ten or twenty years, or a hundred, but I don't have to worry about that right now. I have a team.

And, of course, I have myself.

Tom Jolly is a retired astronautical /electrical engineer who spends his time writing SF and fantasy, designing board games, and creating obnoxious puzzles. His stories have appeared in Analog SF, Daily Science Fiction, MYTHIC, Translunar Travelers Lounge, and a few anthologies, including As Told by Things, and Tales from the Pirate's Cove. His fantasy and SF novels, "An Unusual Practice," "A Game of Broken Minds," and "Touched," are available on Amazon. He lives near Port Orchard, Washington with his wife Penny. You can follow him at Twitter (@tomjolly19) or Facebook (@TJWriter), and find more of his stories on his website: https://sites.google.com/view/tomjolly/home or Amazon author page.

Watchlist

Mark Bilsborough

The current surprise package is Wednesday (Netflix), a Tim Burton series set in the Addams Family universe, together with Catherine Zeta Jones in the iconic Morticia Addams role. On paper the whole idea sounds dreadful and I only watched it after seeing increasingly effusive word of mouth. The Addam's teenage Goth offspring Wednesday is packed off to a Hogwarts style Academy which is full of vampires, werewolves and other supernatural beings and free of 'normals' (with the exception of one of the teachers, played by Christina Ricci, who in a gloriously meta twist played Wednesday in the Addams Family films back in the day). Anyhow, people die and there's a monster on the loose. Wednesday investigates…

Why is this Netflix's biggest hit since *Stranger Things*? And before you ask, it deserves to be. Undoubtedly a lot's down to Tim Burton's quirky weirdness (he does Gothic so well – *Nightmare before Christmas*, *Edward Scissorhands*, *Corpse Bride* etc etc…), but the scripts are tight, the characters interesting and well defined (though J K Rowling should ask for royalties) and, most crucially, the casting is (mostly) spot on, in particular with Jenna Ortega in the role of Wednesday. I think it's true that no-one was hotly anticipating an Addams Family series but I'm willing to bet most of us are eagerly awaiting the next one.

Another blast from the past that no-one (apart form perhaps James Cameron) was hotly anticipating was *Avatar*, now back twelve years after the original (still the biggest grossing movie of all time) with *Avatar: The Way of Water*. Like the first one it's long, it's very pretty and it has a strong narrative about the tensions of colonialisation and the rights of indigenous people. It doesn't tread much new ground but it's nice to pick up where the last one left off – and it seems moviegoers agree. By the time you read this it'll probably be close to (if not at) the top of the all-time global sales rankings (it's currently at number seven with plenty of time to go). But a 77% critics score on Rotten Tomatoes tells a different story – is this hype and expectation over quality? It's hardly *Star Wars: The Phantom Menace* (where expectation was high and reality was dire) but don't expect a classic. Still, there's no such thing as a bad James Cameron film so go see it.

Back on TV we've been watching *The Peripheral on* Amazon, based on a William Gibson novel where people from the near future where our battered world is just about holding it together are pulled into android bodies in the slightly less near future (where things have gone badly wrong and the population has plummeted) for reasons that are never entirely clear, but which involve lots of fighting, high-level rivalries and some broad hints of time travel romance, I liked *The Peripheral* a lot – it's well shot, it's pacy, has great graphics, some solid core ideas and intriguing and engaging characters - but I'm very confused by the narrative (so I'm going to have to read the Gibson novel to see if it makes any more sense) and it ends on a cliffhanger (so we may have to wait years to find out what happened, assuming Amazon doesn't cancel it).

Lastly, I know it's not Christmas anymore but try and catch the *Guardians of the Galaxy Holiday Special* on Disney+ The focus is on Mantis and Drax as they travel to Earth to get Quinn something he's always admired for Christmas – Kevin Bacon. He's chased, kidnapped and, because it's Christmas and you'd expect nothing less, saves the day. Very funny and a good chance to reconnect with these characters ahead of the third Guardians film due out later this year. Oh and catch the other excellent Marvel special too – *Werewolf by Night*

As for 2023, (film) Star Wars is on hiatus, DC is all over the place, a new Star Trek film is but a tantalising dream and a twelve year old movie is the way for sci-fi future. And still no new Battlestar Galactica. But there's loads more to look forward to later this year – on TV the apocalypse drama *The Last of Us* (HBO) is just out, there's more *Mandalorian* (season 3) on the way in March, more *Star Trek* from Paramount (Picard, Discovery, Strange New

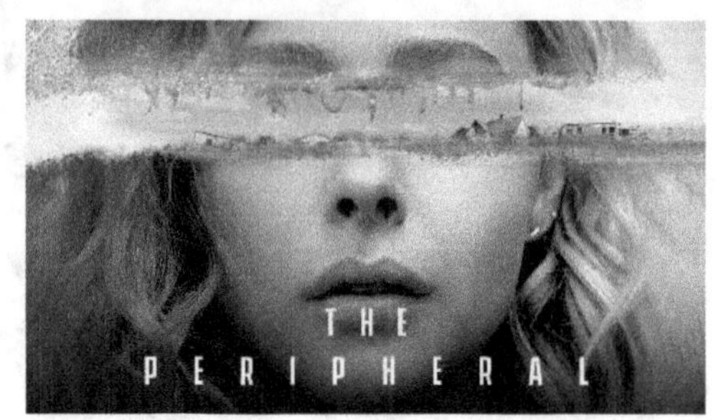

Worlds), and a Disney-boosted big budget for new *Doctor Who* in November. Marvel's giving us the much-trailed Nick Fury (Samuel L Jackson) vehicle *Secret Invasion*, the second season of *Loki* and *Ironheart* and Netflix is going big with a high budget adaptation of Cixin Liu's sprawling *Three Body Problem,* possibly the most famous Chinese SF novel to date. But the one I'm looking forward to most is *Gen V* (Amazon), which is pitched as *The Boys* meets *The Hunger Games,* which sounds immensely watchable.

On film we'll be watching out for *Dune Part 2* (if only to make sense of the first film*), The Hunger Games: The Ballad of Songbirds and Snakes* (which is a prequel to the Jennifer Lawrence films), *Guardians of the Galaxy volume 3,* Adam Driver's *65* (crash landing on strange world – but he's not alone), Halley Berry in *The Mothership* (mystery disappearances, alien objects) and *Ant-Man and the Wasp; Quantumania.* We're also anticipating, with some trepidation, Warner/DC's *The Flash,* which might signal the dying days of the DC Universe (if such a coherent thing exists) mainly to see Michael Keaton reprise Batman (though he's been cut from all the other places he was supposedly due to play Batman in, so who knows).

All in all plenty to look forward to.

Bookworm

Sandra Baker

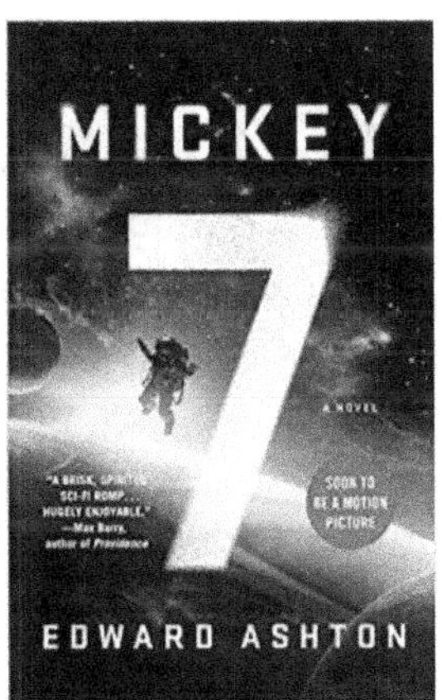

Mickey 7
Edward Ashton

From the first line: "This is gonna be my stupidest death ever," I was intrigued as to where this book was going to go. I already knew that it was an "Intelligent, heartfelt and very funny," book (SciFiNow), but how often is something that is described as 'funny' actually funny?

Spoiler alert: it is a very amusing novel, laugh out loud in many places. It could have gone horribly wrong; it is after all a book about death. However, the story of Mickey 7, a 'disposable employee' on a human expedition sent to colonize the ice world Niflheim is enthralling, quirky and full of tension.

Back on his home planet Midguard, Mickey was the only applicant for the position of an 'Expendable' on the colonising expedition. Hardly surprising, as the job involves undertaking deadly missions in the knowledge that if anything fatal happens, a new 'Mickey' will simply be cloned afterwards. Hence the opening line. By the start of the novel, Mickey has died six times and been regenerated six times. He's quite sanguine about it; he applied for the post simply to get away from a difficult situation back home. However, things start getting weird when he is regenerated even though he hasn't actually died.

It's not long before he comes face to face with Mickey 8. Neither of them want to be melted in some huge incinerator thing (which is what happens to duplicates). So, what follows is a well-crafted story of hide and seek, cat and mouse. And there's an underlying twist: Mickey 7 has found evidence of something sinister on this icy planet that could spell doom for them all.

Mickey is an engaging character, more of an anti-hero at times, but a strong protagonist all the same. The novel explores the concept of immortality through his eyes and through the eyes of the expedition crew, who view and treat him as an abomination.

Ashton is the master of a pacey narrative and you'll find that on every page, he reveals either a peculiar situation or a little surprise that keeps you reading way past your bedtime.

The New Wilderness
Diane Cook

Not 'Sci-fi' but 'Cli-fi,' apparently. So, as you might expect from the title and the genre, this a book that speculates about our relationship with nature – past, present and future.

The set-up sounds like a reality show at first. A group of people opt to live a Neanderthal life, cut off from the rest of the world. We never really know the workings of the project, but we do know that it is the brainchild of Glen, husband of Bea (the protagonist) and father to Agnes (the 'hope for the future'). The family is joined in the wilderness, (an uninhabited and heavily protected area of land, unnamed but I pictured it as the wilds of Montana or Wyoming) by a group of people called 'The Community' who come from all walks of life but with one goal: to escape the dangers of modern society. These dangers are very real for Bea as Agnes had been suffering from life threatening respiratory problems caused by pollution in 'The City' (also unnamed).

There are two main themes: the lengths a mother will go to in order to save the life of her daughter. And the question of whether humans are capable of existing in nature without destroying it.

The story is written from the eyes of 'The Community' and often it seems that the Rangers who patrol the wilderness and instruct the group are just as dangerous as the challenging environment. The Community are told where to trek, where to set up camp and are forced to 'leave no trace' wherever they go. Life is hard, they are living primitively – hunting with flints and spears. Accidents happen, people die. And yet nobody chooses to leave (which they can do, if they desire).

The deterioration of the outside world is mirrored in the changing behaviour of the Rangers towards the group. This cleverly foreshadows the fate of humanity without actually spelling anything out. However, this technique sometimes trips itself up as there are a number of unanswered questions.

This is brutal yet beautiful read. Cook successfully balances the horrors of survival with the splendours of the landscape. It's a compelling story of loss, motherhood and relationships. Interestingly, the writer previously published a collection of short stories titled 'Man v. Nature' in which she explored how people might react to the kind of hardships that exist in the natural world.

Described by reviewers as 'a high-concept dystopia', 'The New Wilderness' was shortlisted for The Booker Prize in 2020. It will make you think, worry, wonder and smile (if a little sadly).

The Daughter of Doctor Moreau

Silvia Moreno-Garcia

H.G. Wells' *The Island of Dr Moreau is* one of the classics of early science fiction – mad scientist doing mad things on a remote island, far from civilisation, turning beasts into men (or at least clever beasts) until it all, inevitably, goes wrong. It followed in the grand tradition of *Frankenstein* and *Dr Jekyll and Mr Hyde* in raising the question: should man play God? As such it's a novel firmly placed amidst the post Darwin debate about evolution, firmly rooted in the age of discovery.

So I was keenly anticipating a return to this madness in the *Daughter of Doctor Moreau,* by Mexican writer Silvia Moreno Garcia. But, sadly, I think she's missed the mark. This book has none of the immediacy of its source and, with its softer, more character based approach, loses its focus on the issues. It's described by the publishers as Mexican Gothic, which is a mashup of thematic approaches that hardly reflects the style of the book, which is a mix of pseudo-Victorian and jarring Americanisms ('candies', kids?).

Part of that is time and context. When *The Island of Dr Moreau* was published in 1896, the book explored new horrors and fears borne of an age when breakneck advances in science and medicine brought fear and optimism in equal measure, but *Daughter* has none of that contextual advantage. Instead, it reads like a pastiche period piece, a gentle what-if reimagining Moreau transplanted into the jungle of the Yucutan Peninsula doing deals with local potentates in order to fund his research on the 'hybrids' who seem way more benign and tamed than the rapidly degenerating beasts of the original.

Eventually, he's found out (which is why Wells set the original in a remote Island – chance are if you do weird abhorrent experiments on human/animal hybrids you're likely to come across people who might find it a problem, so probably best not do it on the mainland, where people might just wander in). Also adding to the drama is his daughter, our point of view character, who for some reason needs regular injections of panther DNA to keep her alive – but which also gives her some exotic special powers. She has a somewhat implausible romance with the much older Montgomery (reimagined from Wells' original, but still an arrogant unpleasant drunk).

This book might have worked for me if the author hadn't invoked the Wells classic. It's a passable (but slow) 19th Century romance with derivative science fiction elements, and I wish she'd changed the names of Moreau and Montgomery to, say, Smith and Jones to weaken the ties – and the inevitable comparisons – to the Wells book. But that aside it's readable if not exceptional.